Stone was immediately captivated by the blue-eyed blonde.

"Your sister is the bride?" he asked.

"Yes." She stopped, adjusted her hair. "I'm Tara Parnell."

Stone was very glad the woman couldn't see his eyes through his sunglasses. If she had, she would have seen the shock and recognition he was sure he couldn't hide. He knew all about Tara Parnell. At least, he knew all about her on paper.

"I'm Stone Dempsey."

"You're the one who was apparently late getting here. Your family gave up on you even coming."

"My family gave up on me a long time ago," he said.

She studied him then, giving him a direct blue-eyed look that became disconcerting in its intensity. Stone almost wanted to look away from her. And yet, he couldn't.

"I've heard a lot about you. But I don't listen to *everything* I hear," she said. She smiled then, which made Stone's stomach do a little dance.

He took off his shades. "You *should* listen. And you should get away from me as fast as you can."

Books by Lenora Worth

Love Inspired

LENORA WORTH

grew up in a small Georgia town and decided in the fourth grade that she wanted to be a writer. But first, she married her high school sweetheart, then moved to Atlanta, Georgia. Taking care of their baby daughter at home while her husband worked at night, Lenora discovered the world of romance novels and knew that's what she wanted to write. And so she began.

A few years later, the family settled in Shreveport, Louisiana, where Lenora continued to write while working as a marketing assistant. After the birth of her second child, a boy, she decided to pursue her dream full-time. In 1993, Lenora's hard work and determination finally paid off with that first sale.

"I never gave up, and I believe my faith in God helped get me through the rough times when I doubted myself," Lenora says. "Each time I start a new book, I say a prayer, asking God to give me the strength and direction to put the words to paper. That's why I'm so thrilled to be a part of Steeple Hill's Love Inspired line, where I can combine my faith in God with my love of romance. It's the best combination."

HEART OF STONE

LENORA WORTH

Published by Steeple Hill Books

STEEPLE HILL BOOKS

Steeple
Hill®

ISBN 0-373-87234-8

HEART OF STONE

Visit us at www.steeplehill.com

Printed in U.S.A.

A new heart I will give you, and a new spirit I will put within you; and I will remove from your body the heart of stone and give you a heart of flesh.

—*Ezekiel* 36:26

To the Surf Sisters—Cindy, Elaine, Sue, Kim, Jackie, Barbara, Julie, Tina, Charlotte, Carla, Pam and Mary Ann—friends for life, sisters forever.

Chapter One

He refused to feel anything.

Stone Dempsey watched as his older brother, Rock, kissed his new bride. They had just married on the beach right in front of the Sunset Island Chapel where Rock preached each and every Sunday, with practically the whole island population and a few tourists witnessing the nuptials. Rock looked happy and so at peace it made Stone's stomach turn. He didn't know why his brother's marriage to Ana Hanson should have him in such a foul mood.

But then, most things kept Stone in a foul mood.

He studied the happy newlyweds behind the cover of his expensive sunglasses. They protected his eyes from the glare of the late-afternoon sun, but mostly they protected his soul from any interlopers. Stone liked watching people, but he didn't like people watching him.

He'd deliberately arrived late, so he stayed back,

away from the crowd, away from his mother who stood dressed in lavender and blue, away from his other brother Clay who had served as best man for Rock's wedding.

At least I was invited, Stone thought, his mind churning like the whitecapped breakers just beyond the shore. The evening tide was coming in. Soon, the wedding party would move to a small reception on the church grounds, underneath the moss-draped live oaks and centuries-old magnolia trees. The party would continue, with just family, later at Ana's Tea Room and Art Gallery.

Maybe he'd skip that part, Stone thought. After all, he had business to take care of—that was the only reason he'd even made an appearance today anyway. His business was in nearby Savannah, and since he had to be in the neighborhood…

As if on cue, Stone's cell phone rang and he turned to hurriedly answer it before anyone else got distracted by the shrill ringing. Not that anyone noticed. Everyone was clapping and cheering his brother and the bride as they headed up the path toward the church.

Stone stepped out of the crowd to duck behind a whitewashed gazebo that had been decorated with trailing flowers and bright netting in celebration of the wedding.

"Hello," he said into the state-of-the-art cell phone, the latest model on the market. "Yes? Great. I'll be there tomorrow morning bright and early. Sounds as if our mysterious seller is finally running out of time."

Stone hung up the phone then turned as he heard a similar ringing nearby. Someone else had received a phone call, too. Someone else had slipped into the gazebo.

And that someone took Stone's breath away.

Watching as she dropped the single white calla lily she'd been carrying onto the gazebo bench, he realized she had been in the wedding party. One of the bridesmaids, maybe? She wore pale baby blue, something slinky with a gathered skirt flowing to just at her knees, and obviously with hidden pockets just right for a cell phone. Her light-blond hair was swept up in an elegant chignon that begged to be shaken and rearranged. And she wore a dainty pearl choker around her slender neck.

Stone hadn't paid much attention to any of the attendants before. But he was paying attention to this one now.

"Hello," she said into the silver-etched phone, her voice as silky soft and sultry as the magnolia blossoms blooming all around them. She was backing up as she talked, but Stone didn't bother to move out of her way. "Yes, I understand. Tomorrow morning. I'll be there. Finally, a face-to-face meeting. Thanks." Her long sigh of relief filled the flower-scented air.

Glancing up the path, she hung up the phone, placed it carefully back in the tiny pocket of her skirts, then turned and ran right smack into Stone.

"Hi there," he said, his gaze hidden behind the safety of his shades.

"Oh, hello. I—I didn't see you there."

"Obviously not."

Surprised, and looking guilty, she grabbed up her flower and stumbled on the wooden gazebo step, but Stone reached out a hand to steady her. "Careful now."

Putting a hand to her hair, she glanced around. "I suppose you think it strange—carrying a cell phone during a wedding."

Stone held up his own phone. "A necessary evil."

She nodded. "Very necessary. I was expecting an important phone call and well...I discovered this dress had pockets, so..."

"So you tucked your phone close because you can't stop working, even for a wedding."

"Even my *sister's* wedding," she said, a trace of what might have been anger at herself causing her to emphasize the words. "I told my assistant not to call *during* the wedding, at least. And I did just turn it back on." That same anger made her look him square in the face, as if daring him to dispute her right to carry her phone. And that's when he saw her eyes, up close for the very first time. They were almost the same blue as her dress. And wide and round. And defiant.

A defiant, blue-eyed, workaholic blonde. A blonde who felt fragile to his touch. Stone was immediately captivated. And cautious. Realizing he was still holding her bare arm, he helped her down the step, then registered what she'd just said. "Your sister is the bride?"

"Yes. Ana Hanson—well, now she's Ana Dempsey—is my sister." She stopped, adjusted her hair again. "I'm Tara Parnell."

Tara Parnell.

Stone was very glad the woman couldn't see his eyes. If she had, she would have seen the shock and recognition he was sure he couldn't hide. He knew all about Tara Parnell. At least, he knew all about her on paper. He hadn't had an inkling, however, about how beautiful and young she was. Stone had pictured a middle-aged, hard-to-deal-with widow.

She *wasn't* middle-aged, but he knew she was a widow, and he had a distinct feeling she *was* going to be hard to deal with even more once she found out why he was here. But then, she didn't have a clue as to who *she* was dealing with either, obviously.

"I'm Stone. Stone Dempsey." He could tell her his name, since he knew beyond any doubt that she didn't know who he really was. He'd been very careful up until now.

"You're Rock's brother." It was a statement, given with a look that hovered between shock and suppressed interest.

Okay, so she now knew that much at least. "One of them. The one who wasn't asked to be a member of the wedding party."

"And the one who was apparently late getting here. Your family gave up on you even coming."

"My family gave up on me a long time ago," he said.

She frowned, then went blank. "Oh, I doubt that. But you were just running late, right? Business?"

"Guilty," he said, without giving any apologies or explanations. "I slipped in the back way."

She studied him then, giving him a direct blue-eyed

look that become disconcerting in its intensity. Stone stared down business opponents every day, but he almost wanted to look away from this woman's all-encompassing blue eyes. And yet, he didn't. He couldn't.

"It's all true," he said by way of defense.

She tilted her head up. "What?"

"Everything you've heard about me, and everything you're wondering about me right now. All the bad stuff about the black sheep of the family. True. Every bit of it."

She smiled then, a soft parting of her wide full lips that made Stone's stomach do a little dance. "Oh, I've heard a lot, that's for sure. But I don't listen to *everything* I hear."

He touched a hand to her arm, then took off his shades.

"You should listen. And you should get away from me as fast as you can."

Summing him up with a sweeping look that told him there was no doubt she wanted to be away from him, she nodded. "Probably a good suggestion, since I'm sure my sister is wondering what happened to me." Then she pushed past him and hurried up the path, her high-heeled strappy sandals crunching against shell and rock.

Stone was glad he'd scared her away, glad she'd had the good sense to heed his warning. Because come tomorrow morning, she would hate him.

Tara Parnell was the business that had brought Stone Dempsey back to Sunset Island.

* * *

"He's very…intense."

Tara turned from the long table where the almond-flavored wedding cake and tropical fruit punch had been set up in the front parlor of Ana's Tea Room, her gaze scanning the intimate group of family and friends that had congregated here after the wedding. Eloise Dempsey reclined on a swing out on the porch, chatting with Tara and Ana's parents, Peggy and Martin Hanson. Clay Dempsey, handsome in a boy-faced way, was sitting on the steps regaling Ana's assistants Tina and Jackie with tales about being a K-9 cop. And that society newspaper columnist, Greta Epperson, was busy taking it all down for next week's *Sunset Island Sentinel.*

Then she saw the man she'd just described as intense, standing apart from the crowd. And she remembered how he'd told her to stay away from him. Or rather, how he'd *warned* her away from him.

Stone Dempsey stood off to one side of the long front porch, his hands tucked into the pockets of his expertly tailored cream linen pants, as he looked out past the oak trees and sand dunes at the sunset-tinged ocean. He'd taken off his navy sports coat and rolled up the sleeves of his cream-and-blue striped oxford shirt. Even in the middle of the crowd, he seemed alone, aloof, but very much aware that Greta was dying to get some exclusive comments from him. He continued to ignore everyone around him, however, including the inquisitive local social reporter.

Ana whirled in her lovely flower-sprinkled wedding dress, a gift from her new husband that had been handmade by eighty-year-old Milly McPherson. Her gaze followed the direction of Tara's stare. "You mean Stone, of course?"

"Of course," Tara replied, reliving how her heart had fluttered when he'd taken off his sunglasses and she'd seen his eyes for the first time. She'd never seen such eyes on a man. They were gray-blue, at once both harsh and gentle, like cut crystal, or perhaps more like shattered crystal. And dangerous. But it wasn't just his eyes.

Stone Dempsey exemplified the kind of controlled power that automatically attracted women. It was a power that spoke of wealth and civility and manners, but it was also a power that held a tempered kind of unleashed energy, a wildness that no amount of designer duds could hide.

"He seems as if he's about to…pounce."

Ana gave her a quizzical look. "I suppose he has to be intense, being such a shrewd businessman. From what Rock tells me, Stone has accumulated a vast amount of money in a short amount of time, mostly through commercial real estate development." Taking a sip of punch, she said, "I'm surprised you haven't heard of him, since you work in the same field. Stone Enterprises is one of the fastest growing companies in the South. He buys up property, resells it to corporations to build subdivisions and resorts, then starts all over again. Rock says he's driven. He works hard, and he plays hard, by all accounts. And has women begging at his feet. Or at least according to the island gossips."

Tara gasped, her mouth dropping open. "I have heard of Stone Enterprises, but that company is way out of my league. I mean, the firm I work for is small potatoes compared to that.'' Pointing a finger, she said, ''So you're telling me that the man standing out there *is* Stone Enterprises?''

''The very one,'' Ana said. ''Stanton Dempsey himself, in the flesh, better known around here by his nickname, Stone. But he likes to keep a low profile.'' She grinned, then whispered, ''Rock and I actually joked about introducing you two, since you both work in real estate, and given how you both seem to love what you do to the point of distraction.'' Ana indicated her head toward Stone. ''So welcome to lifestyles of the rich and famous.''

Immediately recognizing the matchmaking grin on her sister's face, Tara glared at Ana. ''I think I'll pass. Been there, done that, don't recommend it.''

Ana didn't seem convinced. ''C'mon, you know you love the life to which you've become accustomed—the travel, the clothes, the perks of being such a driven, successful person. It just reminded me of you, when Rock was talking about Stone's need to accumulate more money, more material possessions.''

''Do I seem that greedy to you?'' Tara asked, acutely aware that she had indeed been that greedy and obsessed with work and money at one time. But not anymore.

''No, honey,'' Ana said. ''I know you've changed over the months since Chad's death. And I'm very proud of you. Turning back to God, spending more time with the girls—that's so important. They need that kind of structure and stability in their lives.''

''But I was that way once, wasn't I?'' Tara asked,

humiliation coloring her words. "I neglected my daughters, just to make that next big deal." And look where that had gotten her, she thought to herself.

"You have never neglected your children," Ana countered. "You just got caught up in work, Tara. It happens to all of us." Then she smiled, tugged Tara close. "Thankfully, I have Rock now to keep me grounded. And you have your girls. They've enjoyed having you around these last few weeks before the wedding. And so have I."

"I'm glad," Tara said. "And I really am trying to slow things down, to let go of that need to work so much."

Her guilt grating like sand in a sandal, she remembered her cell phone, still nestled in the deep pocket of her dress. And remembered how Stone Dempsey had caught her doing business on that very phone.

She wanted to tell Ana the truth, that she had to work, had to make the next sale, for the very sake of her daughters. But she wasn't ready for that much honesty. Instead, she turned her thoughts back to the intriguing subject still standing outside like a sculptured statue.

Stone Dempsey was obviously a very rich and powerful man, but more infamous than famous, Tara thought. Since he didn't run in the same business circles as her, she couldn't really say how she knew this about him. She just knew, somehow. Besides, she could see it in the cut of his designer suit, in the shape of his sleek golden-brown, too long hair, in the way he walked and talked. The man exuded wealth and power. She knew the type, after all. She'd been married to one.

"He seems to stand around and brood a lot," she told Ana as they both glanced out the big bay window. "He's barely been civil to anyone, including his mother and brothers."

She saw Rock approach Stone now, saw the blank, bored look Stone gave his brother even as he shook his hand and congratulated him. Saw the way Rock turned away, a confused anger in his eyes. It had been much the same when Eloise had spotted Stone earlier and rushed to hug him close. He'd barely allowed his mother to touch him before he'd held her back, his hands on her arms, his expression devoid of any emotion.

"He is different from Rock, and Clay, too, for that matter, that's for sure," Ana said, smiling the dreamy smile of a new bride. "Like night and day. Think you're up to the challenge?"

"What challenge?" Tara asked. "Look, Ana, I'm not interested in Rock's brother."

"Are you sure about that?"

"Very sure."

Ana looked doubtful. "I say go for it, but be careful."

Tara gave her sister an infuriated look. "So are you telling me to go after Stone, or run in the other direction? Honestly, Ana, I'm not ready for a new relationship."

"I'm not telling you anything," Ana said, waving to her husband through the window. "But I do want you to be happy again. You and Stone…well, you might be good for each other.''

Tara didn't see how two overachievers could be good for each other, and she was surprised Ana would even push her in Stone's direction. But then, her sister was too blissful right now to think straight. Ana probably just wanted Tara to feel the way she did.

Tara watched as Rock entered the room and motioned for her sister. Ana walked toward her new husband, a brilliant smile on her face. Rock's own angered expression changed instantly as he gazed at his new wife. They were obviously happy. And Tara was very happy for them. Ana deserved this kind of love, this kind of life.

I had this once, Tara remembered, her eyes still on Stone.

Correction. She'd thought she had true happiness. But it had been one big facade. She'd married Chad Parnell on a youthful whim, thinking she'd love him forever. That had been her first mistake. And throughout the marriage, there had been other mistakes. No more marital bliss for her.

''Mom, why are you staring so hard at that man out there?''

Tara turned to find her oldest daughter, Laurel, standing there with her hands on her hips, her starkly etched brows lifted in a question.

''I didn't realize I was staring,'' she said, her hand automatically fluttering to her hair. ''Where are your sisters?''

''In the kitchen with Charlotte putting out more

shrimp canapés," Laurel said, rolling her eyes. "Can I please take this dress off now?"

"Not until all of the guests are gone," Tara said, her gaze moving over the blue-and-white floral crepe dress Laurel was wearing. All three of her daughters had been in their Aunt Ana's wedding, but Laurel had been the only one to moan and groan about wearing a frilly dress. "Besides, you look lovely. Did Cal notice?"

That brought a smile to Laurel's sulking face. "He said I looked pretty, but I feel like such a kindergartner in this baby-doll dress."

"Well, he's right." Reaching a hand up to cup Laurel's face, Tara added, "And I agree with him. You do look pretty, baby."

"I'm not a baby. I'm almost fifteen," Laurel said, pushing her mother's hand away. "Oh, never mind. I'm going to find Grandma."

"Okay." Tara hid the pain of her daughter's rejection, but since her husband's death a few months ago, she'd gotten used to Laurel's shutting her out. Her daughter blamed her for Chad's death.

And deep down inside, Tara knew Laurel was right to blame her.

"She one of yours?"

Tara whirled to find Stone leaning against one of the open pocket doors, his coat held in his thumb over one shoulder. He stared at her with that same intensity she'd just mentioned to Ana.

"My oldest," she said, turning to busy herself with gathering napkins and punch cups. "And the reason I'm finding more and more gray hairs on my head."

Dropping his coat on a chair, Stone reached out a hand to take the stack of dishes from her. "I don't see any gray hairs."

"Only my hairdresser knows for sure," Tara quipped, very much aware of his touch. When he'd helped her down the gazebo step earlier, she'd felt a kind of lightning bolt moving up her arm. That same jolt was back now, like a current, humming right up to her heart.

Or maybe more like another warning.

"Does your hairdresser charge you a lot for that shampoo?"

Tara felt the magnetic pull of his eyes as they traveled over her hair then came to settle on her lips before his gaze met hers. Again, she got the feeling that he would pounce on her like a lion at any minute. "Drugstore special," she managed to say. "I'm watching my budget these days."

Why she'd said that, she didn't have a clue. Or maybe she did. Tara had dealt with the whims and demands of her materialistic husband, and now that he was dead, she was dealing with the bills he'd left behind. Maybe she just wanted to set things straight with Stone Dempsey right away, so there would be no misunderstandings. So that he'd see she wasn't like him, in any way, shape or form.

But then, what did it matter? Stone would be gone come tomorrow. And she'd be in a meeting that could very well change her life and hopefully take away some of the financial strain she'd been under since Chad's death.

"It smells good," he said, no disdain for her honesty in his eyes or his words. "Maybe I should invest in shampoo stock."

Tara pulled away, dishes clattering in her hands. "Is that how it is with you? Is everything about money?"

"Yes," he said, unabashed and unashamed. "Isn't that how it is with everyone? Isn't everything always about money?"

"You *are* different from your brothers," she said, frustration and anger making her see red. His words sounded so much like Chad, it hurt to think about it. Or the fact that she'd once felt the same way.

Stone took the dishes away again, this time setting them down on a nearby side table. "And you're completely different from your sister."

"Touché," she replied, feeling the sting of his remark just as much as she'd felt the heat of his touch.

"I didn't mean—"

"I know exactly what you meant," she said, moving around the table to get away from him. Stone made her too jittery, too aware of her own shortcomings.

But there he was, right beside her before she could rush out of the room, his hand bracing against the door facing, blocking her way.

"Could you *please* be a gentleman and let me by?" Tara asked, defiance in each word.

"Could you *please* not be in such a hurry to get away?" he countered, a daring quality in the question.

"I'm not in a hurry," Tara replied, lifting her gaze to meet his compelling eyes. "I just think we got off to a very bad start, you and me." Then she held her gaze and leaned close. "And we both know that you don't visit very often around these parts. We probably won't see each other much, in spite of the fact that my sister just married your brother, so what's the point?"

He let that soak in while he took his time searching her face. Tara dropped her eyes, wishing she hadn't said that, but when she looked back up, his expression had turned grim, as if he understood exactly what she was trying to say to him, exactly what she meant.

"Well, I did try to warn you," he said, dropping his hand away as he stepped back.

Then he picked up his coat, turned and walked out into the night.

Chapter Two

She refused to be nervous.

Finally, Tara thought as she paced the confines of the elegant lawyer's office located in what used to be a Savannah town house, she was going to meet the buyer who'd been playing cat and mouse with her over the land Chad had left her. Finally, she was going to get the price she had named, the only price she would accept for the seventy-five acres of land that was now a prime piece of real estate.

And finally, she was going to get the face-to-face meeting she had requested with the buyer as part of the stipulation for the sale. Tara had to be sure that she was doing the right thing by selling off the land that rightfully belonged to her children. She had to see this mystery man in person, to look him in the eye, to know that she wasn't selling out.

Whoever he was, he wanted this land badly. They'd been negotiating since the day she'd grudgingly de-

cided to put the land on the market. Tara knew the
buyer, who was hiding behind some massive corporate logo, wanted the land for the least amount of
money possible, but she also knew what the land was
worth. Situated between the Savannah River and a
small inland bay, this parcel was well suited to an
upscale subdivision and shopping center. If devel-
oped, it had the potential to generate millions of dollars, which was why she had wrestled with letting it
go.

But Tara didn't have near the kind of capital to
develop the land. That would take a lot of money,
and right now she didn't have it, and she was too in
debt to borrow more. What little bit she had received
from Chad's life insurance was almost entirely gone.
No, what she wanted, what she needed now, was
enough money to get her out of debt and set up college funds for her girls.

"That's all I ask, Lord," she said, still unfamiliar
with trying to pray even though she'd been doing a
lot of that lately, thanks to Rock and Ana. "I only
ask that my children be taken care of. I can handle
the rest."

The same way she'd been handling things since
Chad had died.

The door of the office opened, causing Tara to
whirl around. A petite, redheaded secretary in a
striped suit came strutting into the room, her smile
practiced and calm. "They're on their way," the
woman said. "Would you like anything to drink?
Some coffee maybe?"

"No, I'm fine," Tara replied, trying to muster her

own smile. Her nerves felt like ship rigging pulled too tight, but she refused to let that show.

The redhead straightened a few files, then smiled again. "Let me know if you need anything, Mrs. Parnell. My name is Brandy."

"Thanks, Brandy." Tara watched the woman leave, then sank down into a staid burgundy leather armchair, her gaze moving over the busy Savannah street just outside the tall window. Tourists mingled with businesspeople in the tree-shaded square across the cobblestone street, making Tara think she did need something after all.

What she needed was a long vacation from all the worry and stress of juggling the many financial problems Chad had left her with. What she needed was some way of lifting this tremendous guilt off her shoulders. At least her parents were staying with her and the girls for a while, now that the wedding was over and she had brought her family back to their house in Savannah. Her mom and dad loved the girls and wanted to spend time with them before school started in a few weeks. But in spite of having her folks close, Tara still felt so alone.

"Turn to God," Rock had told her after she'd blurted out the truth to him just last week. "Turn to the Lord, Tara. Give some of it over to Him. I'm telling you, it will help you get through this."

Dear Rock. He couldn't even tell Ana about Tara's troubles, since she'd told them to him as her minister. He had to keep that information confidential. Tara had needlessly begged him to do so, but he had assured he wouldn't break her confidence. He'd also urged her to talk to her sister. But Tara didn't want to worry Ana with her problems, not now when Ana had at last found happiness with Rock. Not now, when Ana had just opened her new tea room to an immediate success. Thank goodness that investment was solid, at least. Tara had managed to loan Ana that little bit of money just before Chad's death, just before the dam had burst on her finances. She didn't want Ana worrying about paying her back right now.

She'd do all the worrying. *Turn to God.*

"I'm trying, Rock," she whispered now, her fear so close she could almost taste it. This fear was born of hurt and pain, after finding out her husband had pretty much left her with nothing. It was a feeling of being helpless, of knowing she'd let Chad struggle with the finances all those years while she kept on pretending things were all right between them. She'd busied herself with work and redecorating, endless shopping, with keeping the girls active, with social responsibilities, just to hide her pain. When one charge card ran out, Chad had simply handed her another one. She never questioned him. He'd fixed it. He'd taken care of things.

Well, you didn't do that, did you, Chad? You didn't really take care of anything. And neither did I. And now, her children would have to pay for their parents' mistakes.

Now, Tara was left to deal with the debt collectors. And the shame. Lowering her head into her hands, she said out loud, "Oh, Chad, where did we go wrong?"

"*You* went wrong by trusting your husband in the first place."

Tara lifted her head, the familiarity of that voice causing the nerves she'd kept at bay to go into a spinning whirl of emotion. "You," she said as she sat there, unable to push out of the chair. "You," she repeated, realization dawning on her like a stormy sunrise.

"Me."

Stone Dempsey walked into the room and threw his briefcase on the mahogany table with the smug air of someone who'd just won the lottery. He was followed by Brandy and an entourage of lawyers and accountants, which only made Tara sickeningly aware of how she must look, slumped in the chair in utter defeat.

Well, she wasn't defeated yet. She had something Stone Dempsey wanted. And now that she knew who was behind the bid to buy her precious land, she wouldn't sell it so easily. Not until she was sure she was doing the right thing for her girls.

Rising up, she adjusted her white linen suit and looked across the conference table at him. "You could have told me yesterday at the wedding. You could have given me that small courtesy."

He calmly placed both hands on the table, then stared across at her, making her heart skip. "What, and spoil the happy occasion? I didn't want to do that." His harsh, unyielding gaze moved over her face, then he added, "And besides, as you so graciously pointed out, I probably won't stick around long enough to worry you. So what's the point?"

Anger made her look him straight in the eye. "The point is—*Mr. Dempsey*—that for months now I've been trying to sell my land, and for months now someone, somewhere has managed to squelch every other offer that's been made. That same someone, who refused to be identified, I might add, doesn't want to give me a fair amount for my land, but he sure doesn't want anyone else to get it, either." Taking a calming breath, she leaned across the table, the fire inside her belly giving her the much needed fuel to tell him exactly what she thought of his underhanded tactics. "The point is—you've been evasive and elusive, teasing me with promises all this time so I wouldn't sell the land to someone else, but never really giving me a firm answer regarding my asking price. I don't appreciate it, but there it is." Lifting away, she stood back, her eyes locking with his. "And I don't think I like you, but here you stand." She shot him a look she hoped showed her disdain. "Maybe your family was right about you, after all."

Tara realized her mistake the minute the words shot out of her mouth. Stone didn't move a muscle, but she saw the twitching in his jaw, saw the flicker of acknowledged pain in the shattered reflection of his eyes before they became as glassy as a broken mirror.

She wished she hadn't mentioned his family.

"Leave us, please," he said with a wave of his hand to the stunned group still gathered at the open double doors.

An older, white-haired man wearing a dark suit spoke up. Tara recognized him as the man she'd been doing business with up to now, the go-between, Griffin Smith. "Stone, I don't think—"

"I said leave me alone with Mrs. Parnell, Griffin," Stone replied, his firm, soft-spoken tone leaving no room for arguments.

The room cleared quickly. Brandy gave them a wide-eyed look, then discreetly closed the door.

And then they were left, staring across the table at each other.

Refusing to be intimidated by a man who had deliberately tricked her, Tara once again put her hands down on the cool smooth-surfaced table, then stared across at him, wary, half expecting him to lunge at her.

Stone did the same, his palms pushing into the polished wood as he stared at her. "I tried to warn you," he said, the whisper of the words so low, Tara had to lean even closer to hear him.

"You didn't warn me about *this,*" she said, amazed that he could be serious. "You didn't even bother mentioning this."

"I told you, I didn't want to interfere with the wedding."

"Afraid I'd burst into a fit of tears and make a scene?"

He shook his head. "No. I stayed quiet out of respect for your sister."

That made her back off. But not much. "That was very considerate of you." Turning her head, her thick hair falling across her face, she said, "Did you come to the wedding to purposely check me out?"

He stared at her hair for a minute, making her wish

she could shove it away, then shook his head. "No. I didn't know who you were until you told me your name."

She let that settle, then asked, "Well, why didn't you say something, then? Why didn't you tell me who *you* were? We were away from everyone. You could have explained."

He stepped back, then crossed his arms over his lightweight gray wool suit. "Maybe I was too busy enjoying...getting to know you."

Tara laughed. "Oh, please. That dripping charm might work on socialites, but it won't work on me. You realized who I was and you didn't do anything about it. You probably even figured out what my phone call was about. Guess that gave you a good laugh."

"Did you see me laughing? Am I laughing right now?"

"No," she said, the honest intensity in his eyes making her decide to be truthful herself. "I don't think you're the laughing type. Too busy nurturing that chip on your shoulder."

"You think you have me figured out, don't you?"

"I've seen your kind before."

"Meaning, your husband?"

Remembering his words as he entered the room, she asked, "And just what would you know about my husband?"

Stone opened the leather briefcase he'd brought into the room, then tossed a heavy manila file across the table at her. "I know he owed me money. I know he owed lots of people money. And I also know that you've been frantically trying to hold several of those people off while you work on this land deal. So why don't you do us both a favor and agree to my price. It's a fair market price for that swamp.''

Tara didn't know how to define the anger and hurt coursing through her system. She wanted to direct it at Chad, but he was dead. So she sent it toward Stone, who was very much alive. ''Chad owes you?''

''We had some dealings through my friend Griffin, yes.'' He shrugged. ''Savannah's business community is close-knit. And your husband was a player. Or at least, he was until he let things get out of hand.''

Tara grabbed the file, glanced at the first few documents, then carefully closed it and placed it back on the table. It was all there. All the gory details of the rise and fall of Chad Parnell.

Her heart dropped to her feet as her anger turned into dread. If Chad owed Stone money, then she'd have to practically give him the land. Besides, if she didn't sell it soon, the bank and the creditors would probably seize it anyway. That realization made her sick to her stomach. She leaned on the table again, but this time it was strictly for physical support. ''How much?''

Stone stared at her, his grim expression changing to one of concern before his face became blank. ''That's not important,'' he said at last. ''I'll absorb that in exchange for the land—at the same price I've already quoted you.''

Tara knew he was playing games with her, banking on her emotional turmoil to steal her land away.

"That's awfully generous of you, considering you just called it swampland."

"Part of it is swamp," he said, reverting back to business with a smooth swipe of his hand through his too long hair. "We'll have to haul in dirt and rock, build restraining walls, sea walls. We'll have to build up the foundation, make sure we don't build half-a-million dollar homes in a flood zone. That's going to cost a pretty penny."

"But you still want the land?"

He gave her a long, appraising look. "Yes, I still want the land."

"Why have I never heard of you? Why didn't Chad ever mention you?"

He shrugged again. "Your husband and I never actually met each other. Griffin Smith, who I believe you've been working with, acted on my behalf with your husband. I prefer working as a consultant for other companies, like a troubleshooter, behind the scenes."

"So you can use underhanded tactics?"

He didn't even flinch. "I use wise business tactics. I advise people on how to buy and sell vast amounts of property, and I do the same myself. That's how your husband found me—he needed to unload a few buildings, some warehouses out on the river."

Tara knew about that property—she'd already spent part of that money, too, to pay off some of the charge cards.

"And so you graciously helped him, for a small fee?"

"Actually, it was a rather large fee, which I've

never collected.'' He looked down then. ''We sold the property right before he died, so I held off on collecting my cut. And look, I'm sorry—''

She cut him off with a hand in the air. She didn't need his sympathy. ''So that's when you came gunning for me, right?'' She had to wonder if he'd been watching her all along, and just waiting for the right time to strike.

''I knew of your situation, yes. Then I did some research.'' He stopped, rubbed a hand down his chin while his eyes searched her face. ''I didn't know…about you—that you were Ana's sister. I only knew Chad was married.'' He waited a beat, then added, ''Tara, I only see what's on paper.''

Deciding that statement clearly summed him up, she inclined her head. ''So you heard about the land, saw a good opportunity—on paper—then bided your time until you knew I couldn't hold out any longer. Is that why you finally agreed to meet with me?''

He shifted, and sighed. ''I agreed to meet with you because you were being stubborn. Griffin could have handled the contract, but you kept digging, wanting to know about the company trying to buy your land.''

''You mean Hidden Haven Development Company? Is that just a name you pulled out of a hat or does it have some sort of subliminal meaning?''

''No, it's legitimate. A subsidiary of Stone Enterprises.''

''And you are Stone Enterprises, of course. That much I do know.''

He nodded. ''Normally, I prefer to remain anonymous. It just makes things easier in the long run.''

She nodded. "Easier for you. That way you don't have to face the people you've bullied and taken advantage of."

"I take advantage of situations, not people," he said, and she could see the fire of that conviction in his slate-colored eyes. He actually believed that baloney.

"Oh, good. I feel better already."

"Look," he said, impatience and irritation coloring his words. "Can we just get on with this? Do you want to sell me the property or not?"

Crossing her arms again, she asked in a defiant, split second decision, "What if I've changed my mind? What if I say the deal is off?"

And then, he did it. He pounced.

Pulling her across the table with a hand wrapped around her wrist, Stone brought Tara's face close to his, his shimmering eyes moving over her hair and lips. "Oh, no, darling. It doesn't quite work that way. Because you see, now, I want much more than that land, Tara."

"You're going to have to explain that," she said, her face inches from his. "What else could you possibly want?"

Stone stared at the woman he was holding, his thoughts going back to yesterday, when he'd first met her. That particular encounter had kept him awake most of last night. He'd come so close to calling her in the middle of the night to prepare her, but around 3:00 a.m. had decided it wouldn't matter. He'd probably never see Tara Parnell again after this sale was finalized.

If it was finalized. By the look in her cornflower-blue eyes, that might not be happening anytime soon.

But he wanted to see her again.

And what he wanted right now, right this very minute, was to kiss her. But Stone refrained from that particular need. He had to play this cool. He had to forget about how attracted he was to Tara Parnell and remember the real prize.

He wanted that land. *And* her. But he couldn't tell her that, of course. Not yet, anyway.

"I want us to talk about it," he said, hoping she would stick around long enough for that, at least. "We need to have a calm, rational discussion."

She yanked her arm away, as if disgusted with him. "I am not *calm* and *rational* right now. And I want to get as far away from you as possible."

He didn't blame her. Stone knew he had her cornered. It was how he worked. He negotiated through his lawyers and managers, then he sat back and waited, always silent, always low-key, and always one step ahead of the rest of the pack. It drove people crazy, but it worked. But strangely, today's victory didn't bring him the usual rush of adrenaline he normally got when closing a deal. "I did try—"

Her finger in the air stopped him. "Do not tell me again how you tried to warn me. Nothing could have prepared me for this."

"I'm willing to explain it to you," he said, wishing he *could* explain his need for more money and power, his need to be successful at all costs. "If you sit down and let me bring my people back in, I can show you why this is a fair offer."

She paced the floor, giving him ample time to enjoy the way her crisp suit fit her slender, petite body. He also enjoyed the way she tossed those thick, blond bangs out of her pretty eyes.

Except those eyes were now centered on him.

"Okay," she said, the one word calm and quiet. "Get them back in here. Where do I sign?"

Her defeat floored Stone. Literally. He sank down in his own chair, ran a hand through his long bangs, then glanced up at her. "What? No fight? And to think, I was so looking forward to sparring with you."

She turned then and he would never forget the look in her eyes. Forget disgust. She hated him. Stone could feel it to his very soul. And nothing had ever burned him so badly.

"I don't have any fight left," she said, her words devoid of any emotion. "I have to consider my children." She turned away again.

Don't let her cry, Stone silently pleaded. Although he wasn't sure to whom or what he was pleading.

But she didn't cry. She just wrapped her arms against her stomach, as if to ward off being sick, then turned to face him. "Since you know so very much about my late husband, and me, too, for that matter, Mr. Dempsey, then you probably know that I can't hold out any longer. I've used up most of my assets to pay off the credit cards and the other bills. I've used some of the life insurance to make the house payment, and while I'm trying to sell the house, I still need to buy groceries and clothes for three growing girls, not to mention school supplies and health insurance, so I've sold off everything I could to have some sort of cash flow. But soon that will be dried up, too. And my salary, as nice and cushy as it might seem, won't begin to cover the debts my husband left because my company has threatened downsizing and I won't be getting a raise anytime soon.

"So, you see, I'm tired of fighting. I'm tired of playing games. I need the money you're willing to pay for that land, even though we both know it's worth more than the price you've quoted me. And I need it now. Today." She leaned over the table again, then grabbed a pen, her hand steady in spite of the emotion cresting in her voice. "So, call the lawyers and accountants back in and show me where to sign. I want to get this over with."

Something inside Stone changed. It was a subtle shifting, much like sand flowing through a sieve. It was just a nudge of doubt and regret, coupled with admiration for her spunk and strength, but it pushed through enough to scare him to death. He couldn't go soft. Not now. Not after he'd been working this deal for months.

But he did go soft. Goodness, he wasn't such an ogre that he'd cause a woman's children to go hungry. Was he?

"Look, Tara, we don't have to do this today."

It was her turn to pounce. Tara lunged across the table at him, her blue eyes bright with tears she wouldn't shed, her expression full of loathing and rage. "Oh, yes, we do have to do this today. Because I will not allow you to continue to humiliate or goad me. You've won, Mr. Dempsey—"

"I'm Stone. Call me Stone, please."

She gave the suggestion some thought. "Okay, then, *Stone.* You've won. You can have the land, as long as I never have to see you again. I'll deal with your middleman, and anybody else who wants to do your dirty work, but don't you ever show your face around me again. That has to be part of the deal."

Now Stone actually felt sick. Sick at himself for being so rude and ruthless. He felt deflated, defeated, done in.

By a blue-eyed blond widow who *had* turned out to be very hard to deal with. A blue-eyed blond widow who'd just told him she never wanted to see him again. Only, he *had* to see her again. Now he had to convince her of that, too.

"You're not serious," he said, giving her a half smile full of puzzlement.

"I'm dead serious," she replied, giving him a tight-lipped ultimatum. "I want it in the contract."

Stone got up, pushed at his hair. "You want me to put in the contract that you won't have to ever see me again?"

"That's what I said—but I want it worded—that I don't *want* to ever see you again."

"That won't hold up. You'll have to see me, Tara, to finish up the paperwork, at least."

"Then the deal's off. You did say you like to remain in the background, let other people handle the details. What was it—you prefer to stay anonymous?"

"But that's crazy. Once the papers are signed, that clause won't mean anything. And it won't matter."

"You're right," she said, smiling at last. "It won't

matter then, because *you* won't matter. At all." She rubbed her hands together, then tossed them in the air, as if she'd just washed away a bad stain. "I'll be done with you by then."

Stone felt sweat trickling down the center of his back. This deal had all of a sudden turned very, very sour.

Surprisingly, he wanted it to matter. He wanted to matter to her. And he certainly didn't want her to be done with him just yet. Because he wasn't done with her, not by a long shot. In fact, as the famous saying went, he'd only just begun to fight.

Stone watched her, saw the agitation on her pretty face, but decided he was willing to suffer her wrath just to keep her near. "We're *not* finished here, Tara. Because I've just decided I'm not ready to sign that contract."

Her rage went into double overdrive. Giving him an incredulous look, she asked, "What do you mean?"

"I mean, I want to reconsider this deal. We've waited this long, why not take it slow and think it through?"

"I told you, I want to get this over with."

"Yes, I heard that loud and clear. And I'm asking you to wait. Just one week."

She stomped and shifted, her taupe heels clicking softly against the carpet. "I'm agreeing to your offer on the land. You can't intimidate me or play games with me anymore. What more can you possibly hope to gain by waiting, Stone?"

He came around the table, and unable to stop himself, he pushed at the fringe of bangs falling against her cheekbone. "Your respect," he said. "I'll be in touch."

Then he turned and left the room.

Chapter Three

It had been nearly a week.

Tara stood at the window of her bedroom, looking out over the swimming pool and trees in her lush backyard. It was beautiful, and Chad had been very proud of it, but Tara didn't see the shimmering water of the pool or the tropical foliage that she'd paid a landscaper to plant in her yard.

She only saw red. Because of Stone Dempsey.

He'd said he'd be in touch, but in the four days since she'd met with him, she hadn't heard a word from the man. Even his trusted associate, Griffin Smith, wouldn't return her calls. And she'd called several times. If Stone really wanted to win her respect, he could at least return her phone calls.

But then, maybe he had decided she didn't merit any respect after all. "I guess I blew it," she said aloud, her hands going to her aching head.

"Blew what?" Laurel came sauntering into the

room, the sullen look on her face indicating that her mother had messed up on several things.

Surprised by this unexpected visit, Tara smiled. "Nothing for you to worry about, honey."

Laurel plopped down on a gold brocade chaise longue set before the sliding door leading out to the pool.

"What's up with you?" Tara asked, cautious to not sound too eager.

"I want to go to a concert in Savannah tomorrow night. All my friends are going. Will you take me?"

"What kind of concert?" Tara asked, the price of the ticket already adding up in her brain. The ticket, a new outfit, food. The sum kept silently increasing.

Laurel twisted the strands of a tiny braid she'd worn on one side of her temple all summer, while the rest of her long hair hung down her back. "It's a new alternative rock band. They're awesome. Can I go, please?"

Tara ignored the pain pounding in her head. "What's the name of this awesome new band?"

"The Grass Snakes," Laurel said, hopping up, her hands in the air. "Their latest single—'Out to Get You, Girl'—it's number one this week. I'll just die if I can't go, Mom."

Already, Tara didn't like the tone of this conversation. "And what is the rating on their latest CD?"

Laurel rolled her eyes, her heavily ringed fingers still threading through her braid. "What's that matter? I like them. C'mon, Mom, don't be such a drag."

"I'm not being a drag," Tara replied, familiar with

this conversation. "I'm being a responsible mother. And until I find out what kind of music this awesome new Snake band is playing and if it's suitable for you, I can't agree to let you go to this concert."

Laurel's oval face flushed with anger. "You are so lame! Since when did you start being *responsible,* anyway?"

Hurt by the rage spewing out of her daughter, Tara could only stare. When she finally found her voice, she asked, "What does that mean, Laurel? I'm your mother. I'm trying to do what I think is best."

"Yeah, right," Laurel shouted, her hands on her hip-hugger jeans. "*Now,* Mom. *Now* you're trying to do the right thing. Now that Dad is gone and you've finally realized you have a family—"

At Tara's shocked gasp, Laurel stopped, tears welling in her eyes. "Oh, never mind. It's a dumb band, anyway. I'll just sit at home and mope, the way you do!"

With that, Laurel marched to the door, only to run smack into Tara's mother, Peggy.

"Whoa," Peggy said, her hands reaching up to steady Laurel. "Where are you going?" Seeing the look on Tara's face, she held Laurel with her hands on the girl's slender arms. "What's wrong?"

"It's her!" Laurel said, jerking away to point at Tara. "She's decided to be a real mom, only it's too late for that now."

Peggy watched as her granddaughter charged down the hall and up the stairs to her room on the second floor, then she turned to Tara as they both heard the door slamming shut. "I thought things were getting better between you two."

"Me, too," Tara said, slinking down on the bed. Her voice shaky, she said, "We had such a good talk a few weeks ago, you know, after she ran away with Cal Ashworth."

Peggy sat down next to her. "Honey, they didn't run away. They just fell asleep on the beach."

"Yes, and caused Ana to worry and then hurt her ankle looking for them."

"But…as you said, you worked through that."

"I thought we worked through it," Tara said, looking at her mother's comforting face. Ana looked like their mother. They both had auburn hair and green eyes, whereas Tara took after their father, blonde and blue eyed. "At times, we can talk and laugh, at other times, she reverts back to a little she-monster."

Her mother's knowing green eyes were appraising her now, in the way only a mother's could. "What's wrong this time?"

"She wants to go to some rock concert in Savannah this weekend. I simply wanted to know what kind of songs this bands sings, before I let her go."

Peggy smiled. "Does that sound familiar?"

Tara nodded, wiped her eyes. "I remember, Mom. My freshman year in high school. I wanted to go see some heavy metal band that was playing in Atlanta, and you refused to even consider it."

"You pouted for two weeks."

Tara took her mother's hand in hers. "Yes, and

about a month later, the band broke up. Their fifteen minutes of fame was over.''

''Glad you're not still pouting,'' Peggy said. ''Honey, Laurel will be fine. She's at that age—growing up, hormones going wacky.''

Tara nodded. ''Yes, but it's more than that. She's still so angry at me…because of Chad's death.''

''She can't blame you for that,'' Peggy said, frowning. ''The man died of a heart attack. Granted, he was way too young, but…you didn't know. None of us knew how sick Chad was.''

''Tell that to Laurel,'' Tara said, getting up to pace around the spacious room. ''Mom, she heard us fighting the night before he died.''

''Oh, my,'' Peggy said, a hand playing through her clipped hair. ''Have you talked to her about this?''

''I've tried. We talked a little about it after…after I realized how much Laurel was hurting, and I thought we were making progress. Rock's been counseling her about forgiveness, and letting go of her anger.''

Peggy's expression was full of understanding. ''Well, maybe this outburst is just because you won't let her go to the concert.''

Tara shook her head. ''You heard what she said. Laurel doesn't believe I'm a good mother. And maybe she's right.''

''No,'' Peggy replied, coming to stand by her. ''You have always been a good mother. You know, we all slip up now and again. The important thing is to not keep making the same mistakes. I don't think you're going to let anything come between you and your children, ever again.''

"No, I'm not,'' Tara said, wishing she could tell her mother all of her worries. But then, her mother would just worry right along with her, and she didn't want that. "Thanks, Mom,'' she said instead. "I'm so glad you and Daddy decided to spend this week here.''

"Me, too, honey.'' Peggy gave her a quick hug, then said, "Oh, by the way, Ana called earlier while you were out. She invited us to come to the island Saturday. The church is having a picnic on the grounds. Some sort of anniversary celebration.''

Tara groaned. "Oh, yes. The church is 230 years old. Can you imagine that? I'd forgotten all about the celebration.''

"Amanda wants to go,'' Peggy said, her hand on the door. "And I think Marybeth does, too.''

"But I bet Laurel won't like it, as compared to going to a concert in the city.''

"Cal will be there,'' Peggy pointed out. "You might try reminding her of that.''

"Good idea,'' Tara replied. "And a good reason to keep her from attending that concert.''

And a good reason for Tara not to dwell all weekend on why Stone Dempsey hadn't returned her phone calls.

"She's called twice today, Stone.''

"Let her keep calling,'' Stone replied, his gaze

scanning the computer screen in front of him. "That land's not going anywhere."

He stopped reading the screen, aware that his executive assistant, Diane Mosley, was still standing there, staring at him with the precision of a laser light.

"What?" he finally said, closing the laptop to glare up at the woman who had been by his side since he'd first opened a storefront office, straight out of college ten years ago, in an older section of Savannah's business district.

Diane was close to fifty, her hair platinum blond and short-cropped, her eyes a keen hazel behind her wire-rimmed bifocals. Pursing her lips, she tapped a sensible-shoed foot on the marble floor. "Why are you tormenting that poor woman?"

Stone felt the wrath of Diane's formidable reprimand. But he didn't dare let it show. They had an understanding, his dependable, loyal assistant and him. She was really the boss, but he really didn't want to admit that. So they pretended he was the boss. It worked fine most days. Unless she started mothering him or pestering him.

Like now.

"I am not tormenting Tara Parnell. I have every right to go back to the drawing board regarding that piece of property. After all, we're talking millions of dollars here. I want to make sure I have all my ducks in a row."

"I understand about your little ducks," Diane said, her steely gaze unwavering. "What I don't understand is why you've seemed so edgy since meeting with Mrs. Parnell. If I didn't know better, I'd think she got the best of you.''

Stone glanced at the grandfather clock centered between two multipaned windows, then deciding it was close enough to quitting time, loosened his silk tie. Since he didn't want to go into detail regarding his wildly variable feelings about Tara Parnell, he said, ''No, actually, she brought out the worst in me, which is why I'm reconsidering this whole deal.''

He'd planned an overall assault. Flowers, candy, the works. He'd planned on forcing Tara to spend time with him over the last week. But somehow, that planned tactic had gone by the wayside. Each time he remembered how she'd looked at him, with all that hate and disgust, he got cold feet and decided he'd do better sticking to business and playing hardball. He'd be much safer that way, less vulnerable to a counterattack.

''You aren't going to let the land go, are you?'' Diane asked, shifting her files from one arm to the other. ''Stone, you've been eyeing that land for months now.''

''Yes, I have,'' he admitted. Chad Parnell had let it slip about the land he'd bought dirt cheap from a family friend years ago, land he'd been sitting on until the right time to sell. Only, Chad had died before being able to turn a profit on the land. But Stone had remembered the land, and everything had fallen into place. ''No, I'm not going to let go of the land, Diane. But if it will make you stop glowering at me like I'm an ugly bulldog, I'll tell you why I'm holding off.''

Diane settled one ample hip against the solid oak of his big desk, then lowered her eyeglasses. "Do tell."

"Don't mention this to Griffin," Stone said. "But I've reached a conclusion, one I think will be beneficial to both Mrs. Parnell and me."

"What's wrong with you?" Ana asked Tara the following Saturday.

They were sitting in lawn chairs behind the tiny Sunset Island Chapel, overlooking the docks of the bay and Sunset Sound to the west. Out over the sound, hungry gulls searched the waters for tasty tidbits, their caws sounding shrill in the late-afternoon air. A fresh-smelling tropical breeze rattled through the tall, moss-draped live oaks, its touch swaying the palmetto branches clustered here and there around the property. Behind them, near an arched trellis, a gardenia bush was blossoming with sweet-scented bursts of white flowers.

"I'm okay," Tara replied, her dark sunshades hiding the truth she felt sure was flashing through her eyes. "Just another fight with Laurel."

"Oh, yes, that," Ana said. "I heard." Taking a quick look around, she added, "Well, she seems to be over not going to the concert. Look at her." She inclined her head toward the docks.

Tara leaned up, squinting, then saw her daughter and Cal, sitting on one of the many wooden docks lining the bay where luxury yachts shared slips with smaller, less impressive sailboats, shrimp boats and motorboats. They were talking and laughing, their hands waving in the air. Not far away, a long brown pelican stood sentinel on an aged pier railing.

"He is a very nice boy," Tara said, lifting a hand toward Cal. "A good influence on Laurel, if he'll stick to the rules and not sneak off into the night with her again."

"Oh, I think Cal's learned his lesson on that one," Ana replied. "His father made him work that particular crime off, sweating and painting all summer."

"What about his mother? I never hear anyone mention her."

"She died when he was seven. It's sad, really. Don has sisters and brothers who help him with his children. Cal's got two older sisters, too, who watch out for him."

"That explains a few things," Tara said, her heart hurting for her daughter. "Maybe that's why Laurel's drawn to Cal. You know, losing a parent."

"Maybe." Ana sat up, waved to someone she knew. "Oh, I need to talk to that woman. She commissioned a small sculpture from Eloise, to be delivered to my shop. I want to tell her it's ready."

"Okay," Tara said, closing her eyes as she settled back to let the sun wash over her. "I'll just lie here and vegetate a few more minutes before I find the strength to sample more of Rock's wonderful barbecued ribs."

"Yes, my husband does have nice ribs," Ana quipped, slapping Tara playfully on the leg as she hopped up.

Tara didn't bother opening her eyes. The sun felt good on her legs. She'd worn a black gauze sarong skirt, lightweight and cool-feeling, with a knit red-and-black flower-splashed sleeveless top. Lifting at the skirt, she kicked off her black leather thong sandals and tried for the hundredth time to relax.

But all she could think about was her money woes and the fact that her oldest daughter thought she was a horrible mother. She'd prayed that things would turn around for her family, hoped that God would see fit to give her another chance. But she still had doubts. She still needed answers, guidance, assurance.

And maybe some solid health and life insurance.

Help me here, Lord, she thought. *Help me to make my life better, for the sake of my children.* She'd tried so hard all summer, working on two different land deals. But this was about more than money. Tara needed the money those deals could bring, but she also needed to spend time with her children. She'd taken way too much time off already, and her bosses weren't too happy about that. *What am I supposed to do, Lord?*

A shadow fell across Tara's face.

Annoyed, she opened her eyes to find Stone Dempsey standing over her. She didn't know why her heart seemed to sail off like a ship leaving the cove. She didn't understand why he looked so very good in his stark white polo shirt and olive-khaki pleated slacks. Tara only knew that she needed some answers. From God and Stone Dempsey.

"Me," he said, as if to answer the one question she was about to ask.

"You," Tara replied. "What are you doing here, Stone?"

"I came bearing gifts." He tossed a bouquet of fresh cut flowers onto her lap.

Tara sat up, sniffed the lilies and roses. "How did you know where to find me?"

"I have ways of finding people," he said. "Especially when I'm in the middle of negotiating a contract."

Tara imagined he knew every move she'd made since they last talked, which was a bit too unsettling. But she refused to let her qualms show. "Well, you obviously aren't too concerned, since you refused to return my calls."

He took that in, glanced out at the harbor, then lifted his shades to stare down at her. "I've been busy coming up with another plan. And I'm here because I hope we can renegotiate."

The heat from his eyes hit her with all the warmth of the sun, causing Tara to shift and straighten her skirt. "Meaning the contract, of course?"

"Among other things."

Tara thought she knew what other things he wanted to haggle over, but she didn't dare think about that now. "What's to renegotiate? You've named your price and I've accepted it."

"With a certain stipulation, if you'll recall?"

"Yes, I recall. I never wanted to see you again. But I need to sell that property, so in spite of how I feel, I've tried calling you to discuss things. You obviously aren't in a big hurry for that land, after all.''

"I'm in a hurry," he said, leaning down so close she could smell the subtle spice of his aftershave. "But I can be patient, too.''

"What does that mean?" Tara said, trying to get up out of the low chair.

He reached down and pulled her out of the chair with one hand on her arm, then brought her close, his gaze sweeping her. "Careful now.''

Why couldn't she be graceful around him, at least, Tara wondered. Because the man flustered her, plain and simple.

Not so plain and not so simple.

"I told you, I'm through playing games," Tara said, trying to move around him, her flowers clutched to her side.

"I'm not playing, Tara." The look in his eyes washed over her like a warm, shimmering ocean wave, leaving her both languid and alert. "Have dinner with me.''

"Absolutely not.''

"I won't take no for an answer.''

"Oh, yes, you will. Because it's not going to happen.''

"Tara, what's going on with you and Stone?" Ana asked Tara later that night. "He's called here three times." Before Tara could reply, Ana clapped her hands together. "Did you take me up on my suggestion? Is that it? Are you going out with Stone, like on a date?''

''Oh, please!''

Tara sat across the massive kitchen counter of the tea room, folding napkins for tomorrow's after-church brunch crowd. The girls and her parents were down on the beach with Rock and Cal, leaving the two sisters alone in the big Victorian house that served both as Ana's tea room and art gallery on the bottom floor and Ana and Rock''s home on the second and third floors. Business had been so good at the quaint restaurant, Rock and Ana hadn't really had a proper honeymoon—just one weekend together alone in this big old house. But Ana didn't seem to mind. She was happy. Too happy to understand this problem with Rock's brother.

Which was why Tara had debated telling Ana about Stone. Now she didn't have any choice. He'd called here, asking for Tara. Luckily, Rock hadn't answered.

''Oh, please, what?'' Ana said, her hands on her hips before she went back to her bread dough. ''Tell me, Tara. I mean, you two must have really clicked at the wedding, so why are you holding out on me?''

''It's business,'' she said finally. ''Stone is trying to buy my land.''

Ana stopped stirring bread dough, her mouth dropping open. ''That land near Savannah that Chad bought all those years ago?''

''Yes.'' Tara nodded, folded another napkin, then stopped, looking down at the counter. ''He wants to develop it into an upscale gated residential community, complete with shopping centers and restaurants near the river.''

Ana dropped her spoon to stare at her sister. ''That could mean a lot of money, right?''

Tara nodded again. ''He's offering me a lot, yes, but not as much as I'd hoped to get.''

''And when did all of this come about? Certainly not at the wedding?''

Tara kept her eyes down. ''No, we just met at the wedding. Look, it's a long story—''

A knock on the back door stopped Tara in midsentence. ''You've got some explaining to do,'' Ana said underneath her breath before she opened the door.

Eloise Dempsey whirled in, carrying a yellow-colored sealed folder in her hand, her gaze hitting on Tara. ''Oh, good, you're here. I'm supposed to deliver this to you.''

''What is it?'' Tara asked, surprised to find the famous sculpture artist playing postmistress.

Eloise gave her a wry smile, then shook her head, her feathered dreamcatcher earrings shimmering and shimmying as she moved around the long counter to give Ana a quick peck on the cheek. ''Well, it's the strangest thing,'' Eloise said, her eyes back on Tara. ''My son Stone came to pay me a rare visit this evening. We had a nice dinner and then he said he needed me to do him a favor.''

Tara's heart picked up tempo, while her sister picked up an obvious interest in the conversation. ''What else did he say?'' Tara asked, her eyes locking with Ana's.

"He said to tell you, actually to tell all of us, we're invited to a private dinner party next month, at his home here on the island—Hidden Hill."

"What type of dinner party?" Ana asked before Tara could say a word. "I mean, that old mansion isn't in any kind of shape for a party."

"Oh, a black-tie benefit for the lighthouse." Eloise clapped her hands together. "He implied it was by invitation only. And I think he's going to hold it in the garden, in spite of how bad the place looks. I believe we'll all receive our formal invitation in about a week or so."

Ana smirked, then rolled her eyes. "So Stone couldn't come down to the fair we held last month, to mingle with the little people?"

"I guess not," Eloise said. "But he wants to do his part—make a contribution toward the restoration."

"Of course he does," Ana said, making a face to Tara behind Eloise's back. Then, as if she regretted being so cynical, she added, "That is good news, Eloise."

Eloise nodded. "Yes, and I'm so glad I was invited. And you and Rock, too, of course, Ana. Stone was very evasive about the whole thing. An exclusive crowd, I suppose."

"You think?" Ana asked, shaking her head.

"I think," Eloise replied, calm as always, "that our Stone has come home, at last. I think his brother's wedding made him realize that he needs to settle down. I also think he needs our understanding and forgiveness.''

''You're right, of course,'' Ana said. ''And I'm sorry if I sounded a tad suspicious. I mean, I'm the one who's been encouraging Rock to try for a better relationship with his brother, so I shouldn't be doubtful.''

Eloise smiled softly. ''Stone hasn't given us very much reason to think otherwise. Until now.''

''Yes,'' Tara agreed, her eyes on the fat envelope laying on the counter. ''But what's that got to do with me? And what's in this envelope?''

''I don't know, dear,'' Eloise said, her keen gaze centered on Tara. ''Why don't you open it and find out?''

Chapter Four

Tara eyed the envelope as if it were a snake.

"Open it," Ana said, her curiosity obvious in the wide-eyed look she gave her sister.

Tara reached for the envelope, turned it over. "I don't understand what this could be. And why Stone would have you deliver it."

Eloise shot Ana a quizzical look that Tara couldn't miss. "Stone and I had a good talk at the wedding the other day," Eloise said. "He promised he was going to come around more. Then, tonight he told me he was going to stay here on the island for a few weeks. He's renovating that old mansion, so he wants to be close to the work. He's a details man, my Stone. Other than learning he's going to be here a while, I'm stunned and clueless."

"So is this one of those details?" Tara asked, wondering just how much Stone really had told his mother about her. And wondering what Eloise wasn't telling her.

"I don't know," Eloise said with an eloquent shrug. "I only know that my second son seems fascinated by you, dear."

Ana cleared her throat and began briskly kneading her bread dough. "Maybe it's about the land, Tara."

Rock came into the kitchen right as the words left Ana's mouth. "What land?" Glancing down at the bright envelope, he saw the label from Stone Enterprises, then asked, "What's that?"

"Hello, Rock," Eloise said as he leaned down to absently kiss her cheek. "I just delivered this to Tara, from your brother, Stone. He's staying at Hidden Hill for a while."

Tara winced. She didn't want to bring Rock into this. His relationship with his brother wasn't the best on a good day. "It's business," she said, her smile weak and shaky.

"What kind of business do you have with my brother?" Rock asked, his expression wary.

"She was just about to explain that to me when Eloise brought this in," Ana said, pointing to the package.

Tara felt the scrutiny of everyone in the room. Taking a deep breath, she said, "I guess I'd better tell all of you everything, from the beginning."

Rock sank down on a bar stool. "That might be wise."

Tara touched a finger to the package. "I put some land on the market a few months ago—the land Chad left me in the will."

"Near Savannah, right?" Rock said, nodding.

"Yes, centered between a tributary of the Savannah

River and a marsh and pond,'' Tara told him. "Chad always wanted to build a house out there, a weekend retreat. Of course, that can't happen now, so I decided to sell the land.''

"And Stone wants to buy it?'' Rock guessed, his vivid blue eyes studying her face.

"Yes. About a month ago, I got a nibble on the land, from a man named Griffin Smith. He named a price, but I held off. I thought I could get more money for the land.''

"But you can't?''

She shook her head, her gaze on Rock. "I don't think so. Anyway, I held out as long as I could, but the day of the wedding I got a call confirming a face-to-face meeting with the prospective buyer, the man Griffin Smith represented—a man who had been very secretive and hard to pin down.''

"My brother,'' Rock said, the statement confirming his resentment toward Stone. "That's so like Stone.''

Tara nodded. "I had no idea I was dealing with Stone, not even at the wedding. He never indicated it, but he recognized who I was as soon as I told him my name.'' Lowering her gaze, she added, "Of course, he didn't bother telling me who he was, until the meeting the day after the wedding.'' In his defense, and against her better judgment, she said, "He didn't want to disrupt the wedding.''

Rock snorted, rolled a hand down his face. "He didn't want to make a scene? I doubt that. More like he didn't want us to find out what he was up to.''

"Now, Rock—'' Eloise began, only to have her son hold up a hand.

"I know, Mother, I know. Stone has the best of intentions."

Ana Tara shot her husband a warning look, then placed her bread into a baking pan. "So…Stone and you are trying to reach some sort of agreement about the land, Tara?"

Tara rubbed a hand on her throbbing temple. "At the meeting, once I realized who he was, I agreed to his price. But I was upset. I told him I never wanted to see him again."

Rock smiled at that. "I reckon that rankled him."

"It did," Tara admitted. "He backed off the contract, and now we're back in negotiations."

"So what's this?" Rock said, holding up the envelope.

"I have no idea." Tara took it from him. "Let's get this over with."

"Maybe it's the agreement contract," Ana said, leaning close as Tara tore open the sealed package.

Tara took the thick, bound papers out of the package, then started reading. "It is a contract," she said, her eyes scanning the pages. Then she stopped reading, her gaze flying to her sister. "It's not the original contract."

"What's the matter?" Ana asked, her hands holding to the counter.

Tara couldn't believe what she was seeing on the page in front of her. "This can't be right."

"Can you tell us, or should we just mind our own business?" Eloise asked, clearly hoping Tara would share all.

Tara flipped the contract pages over so no one

could see the contents. "I'm sorry. I can't discuss this with any of you. As I said, it's a business decision, between Stone and me." Then she looked at Rock. "But I can say that your brother is crazy if he thinks I'll actually go for this—this deal."

"Stone isn't crazy," Rock said. "He's very shrewd and completely ruthless. Be careful, Tara."

"Oh, I'm going to be very careful," Tara said, heading for the hallway. Then she whirled to face Eloise. "Did you say he's at Hidden Hill?"

"Why, yes, but—"

"Good. Then I can see him tonight and settle this once and for all."

"Settle what?" Ana asked, her hands falling to her side in frustration. "Tara, why can't you talk to us?"

Tara headed for the stairs to change. "Because this is something I have to take care of myself. I'll explain later."

After she confronted Stone Dempsey.

If he wanted her respect, he'd failed miserably in his attempt to show her that. She'd never agree to this kind of manipulation.

Never.

He'd never before wanted to see a woman so badly.

Stone turned from the lower terrace of the big mansion he'd bought a couple of years ago, feeling restless and caged within the confines of the stucco-and-stone walls of Hidden Hill. Staring up at the muted light shining through the doors he'd flung open from the massive drawing room, he wondered why he'd come back here.

He had planned to stay away, to stay in the city until the renovations were complete. The old house needed work from the ground up. It was literally falling apart, its thick stone walls straining and craning underneath the weight of close to a century of storm winds and salt air.

And yet, Stone loved the house.

He loved the twenty-six rooms and the many terraces and steps of the house, even when he remembered having to work here as a teenager, helping with the enormous grounds, helping with the never-ending maintenance such a house required. He hated those memories, even as he loved the house.

He turned toward the sound of the ocean crashing against the shore down below, closing his eyes as he remembered everything bad about Hidden Hill.

A wealthy Northern business tycoon named Thorgood Sinclair had owned the home back then. It had been passed to Thorgood from his millionaire father, who'd built it as a family vacation retreat back in the twenties. Thorgood had rarely stayed at the house. But Stone remembered Mr. Sinclair's fancy wife and three children. The two boys, about the same age as Stone, had taunted and teased him as he sweated away in the yards. The daughter, Ramona, had flirted with him, driving him crazy, while she dated the rich boys she brought down from New York each summer. Stone had taken a lot of heat from the beautiful young lady of the manor.

Well, now he was the lord of the manor. He could hire as many groundskeepers and maintenance men as he needed to turn this place back into the showcase it had once been. And it had given him great pleasure to seize the crumbling house from a washed-out, near bankrupt Thorgood Sinclair, Jr. Junior hadn't remembered who Stone was at first. But by the time the ink had dried on the sale, Junior had not only remembered, he'd sunk down in a chair to stare after Stone as he'd walked out the door with a smug smile on his face. Since the day he'd stood on this very terrace listening to the beautiful Sinclair children frolicking in the pool, Stone had vowed to come back rich and successful himself. And since the day the Sinclairs had put the house up for sale, Stone had dreamed of renovating this old mansion.

Tonight, that dream was very near.

Except that tonight, the dream seemed hollow and lacking. And Stone felt very much alone in the house on the bluff.

Because of her.

Tara Parnell's image shot through his mind as if illuminated from the once beaming glow of the nearby old lighthouse. She'd refused to have dinner with him, and Stone wasn't used to being refused.

So he'd tried another tactic—one she'd probably find just as underhanded as his other modes of operation. He'd sent his mother as envoy, with the one thing that would get Tara's attention.

A revised contract.

Now, he would wait. But he didn't want to wait. Stone was ready for the fight, welcomed the battle he knew was coming. It was the only way to get to see her again. Even if it meant she would be thoroughly angry with him.

* * *

Tara was so angry, she could barely see to find the secluded gate leading up to the big square mansion. Stopping the car at the end of the long, tree-shaded drive, she stared up at the imposing house, taking a minute to calm herself.

The old mansion was impressive. The stark golden and bronzed stone walls stood out in the moonlit night, while a solitary light from a second floor room seemed to be the only illuminated object inside the decaying walls.

Was that where he was waiting? she wondered as she got out of the car and slammed the door, the roar of the ocean matching the roar of slow rage building in her mind. Holding on to the skirts of her flowing sundress, Tara wound her way up the cracked steps leading to the second level terrace. The wind picked up as she moved, causing her hair to lift out around her face. Impatiently, Tara brushed the hair away as she hurried up the stairs toward that light.

As she reached a small landing, she stopped to look toward the terrace. And that's when she saw him. He was waiting, all right. He stood there, as solitary and sad as the house, his hands in the pockets of his trousers, his face in the shadows.

Clutching the contract with one hand, Tara dashed up the remaining stairs, her eyes scanning the construction scaffolding and various tools scattered about the grounds and house. She hated being so predictable, but if Stone wanted to see her, then this latest trick had worked remarkably well in getting her here.

She'd tell him off, tell him no, then leave with some dignity intact, she hoped.

Gasping, she reached the terrace then stopped to breathe deeply. She wouldn't give him the satisfaction of seeing her rattled. But when Stone turned to face her, the look in his crystalline eyes only added to Tara's woes.

It was not the smug, ruthless, victorious look she had expected. Stone was looking at her as if he wanted to pull her into his arms and kiss her.

That look, that all-consuming, all-encompassing inspection that swept her from head to toe, caused her heart to beat in a panicked, trapped effort. Stone looked ready to pounce at any time.

"You're here," he said, as if in awe of the fact that she was standing ten feet away.

"Did you really expect me to just sign this?" Tara asked, regaining control of her heart and her head as she stalked toward him, the contract crushed in her hand.

"Yes," he said, the one word calm and calculated. "It's a good compromise, don't you think?"

"I think you're trying to manipulate me," Tara replied, her eyes scanning his face. "What happened to the original contract?"

"I tore that one up."

"Did it ever occur to you to discuss this with me, before you destroyed the other contract?"

"No."

The wind lifted his hair away from his brow, making him look like a golden lion standing there. Deciding she needed to quit imagining Stone as some jungle cat, Tara advanced a step. "I won't sign this, Stone. In fact, you can just forget the whole thing. I'll find another buyer for my land."

"Do you hate me that much?" he asked, his hands still in his pockets as he rocked back on his expensive loafers.

"I don't know you well enough to hate you," Tara admitted, "but from what I do know, I don't like you very much right now."

He pushed at his hair, looked off toward the distant shore. "Tara, this is a good deal. You told me you had to think of your children. Well, this way—"

She tossed the contract at him. "This way, you win, Stone. You get the land...and...the rest, well, that's charity. And I'm not so destitute that I'll take charity yet, especially from the likes of you."

She watched as he leaned down to pick up the contract. "It's not charity. I am not a charitable man, or haven't you noticed that?"

Tara waved a hand in the air. "All the more reason to suspect you. Why would you want this? Why are you being so—"

"Nice?" He came so close, she could see the perfect shape of his wide lips, could feel the heat from those shattered eyes that refused to stop staring at her.

"You want to give me a signing bonus," she said, stating the terms of the contract, "and then make me a partner in the development corporation for this project." Groaning, she added, "Stone, you're offering to pay me almost exactly the amount of money I need to get out of debt, and you're willing to give me a job, at a salary that will more than pay my bills, and make me a partner? I think, considering the first offer you made, that yes, this is charity, and yes, it's way too nice. You obviously have some other motive.''

In a move that had her back against the cold bricks of the terrace wall, Stone tossed the contract on a nearby wrought-iron table, then pulled Tara into his arms. ''And what if I do have another motive?''

She couldn't move, couldn't find her next breath. ''I don't like this,'' Tara managed to whisper. ''I don't like—''

''Me,'' he finished for her just before his mouth came down on hers. It was a tentative kiss, completely out of character for a man who obviously took what he wanted when he wanted it. The kiss was soft and quick, like a butterfly tickling against her lips, but it left a definite impact on her heart. Then he lifted his mouth, his eyes holding hers. ''You don't like me. I think we've established that much. So because you don't like me, you're refusing my offer? Not a very wise business decision, Tara.''

Tara found the strength to look him in the eye. ''I don't take charity, Stone.''

''It's not charity,'' he said, his hand moving over her cheekbone. ''It's a good deal.''

''For you?''

''Especially for me. This way, I don't have to honor that first contract—you know, the part about you never wanting to see me again.''

''I still feel that way,'' she told him, even while her lips still tingled from his touch. Closing her eyes, she willed his soft, tender fingers on her face to stop making her feel things she didn't need to feel. "I can't do this, Stone."

His hand lifted her chin. "Open your eyes and tell me why you can't."

Tara did as he said, her eyes flying open to find him right there, his face inches from hers. "Because I don't trust you," she admitted.

Stone backed away as if she'd slapped him. And Tara immediately felt raw and exposed, standing there in the misty night wind.

"No respect, no trust," he said, the words hitting her as he tossed them over his shoulder. "I've really got my work cut out for me."

Tara hated the trace of regret in his words. But she had to stand firm. "Can't we just go back to the original deal? I'm willing to take a cut and accept your offer now."

"Rather than having to deal with the likes of me?"

He still had his back to her, and Tara felt the pull of that broad back, felt the need to touch him, nurture him, tell him she understood. But she didn't understand.

"Look," she said, letting out a long sigh, "this would be very awkward. I mean, I'm Ana's sister and you're—"

"The black sheep brother," he said, whirling around, his eyes flashing like shards of white fire. "My reputation precedes me."

"I don't want to make things difficult for Rock and Ana," she tried to explain. "They just got married. They don't need us complicating their lives."

"Oh, no," he said, raking a hand through his hair.

"My brother is so noble and good, so sanctimonious and pure. We can't mess with that, can we?"

"You're wrong about Rock," Tara said, wanting to defend her friend. "He is a good man, and he loves you."

"Oh, really?"

"Yes, really. He talks about you and Clay all the time. He mentioned his family a lot, when he helped me sort through my problems."

"I'll just bet he did."

"He's working on some of his own issues, too, from the past. I don't want to complicate that."

"And you owe him now, right? So you don't want to add to those problems by agreeing to come and work for me."

"Yes, I owe Rock, at least my consideration," she said. "He's brought my life around." She turned to look out over the horizon. Off in the distance, she could see the white-and-red stone of the old lighthouse, and beyond that, the dark, rolling sea. "Rock has shown me how to pray again, how to turn to God for help."

Stone came to stand by her then, his hands digging into the thick terrace railing. "Well, since you've got Rock and God, you certainly don't need me, right?"

"I didn't say that," Tara replied, her gaze touching on his face. He looked as if he'd been carved and shaped, like one of his mother's sculptures. And she wondered what had made him such a hard man. "What I need is to earn a good living for my children. What I need is some peace and quiet, some semblance of order and calm in my life. And I don't think accepting the terms of your offer would bring me that.''

"You're afraid of me," he said, pivoting to touch a hand to her arm. "Just be honest, Tara, and admit that, at least.''

She nodded. "Yes, you do frighten me.''

"I'm offering you enough money to more than take care of your girls," he said, the words echoing out over the night. "Why would you turn that down?''

Tara didn't pull away. Instead, she turned to touch a hand to his face. His skin was soft and warm, a sharp contrast to the hard-edged look in his eyes. "Because over the last few months, I've found out life is about more than money. I know we need it to survive, and I could use enough to get out from under the debts Chad left me, but I have to do it my way this time. I lost control completely, being married to Chad. I won't ever let that happen again.''

Stone leaned into her touch, then took her hand and kissed the inside of her palm. "Is that what this is all about? Are you afraid you'll lose control with me, Tara?''

Tara knew the answer to that question already. She felt it in his touch, in his eyes on her, in the way his kiss had made her come alive. "Yes," she said.

Then she turned and ran back down the steps.

When she reached her car, Tara looked back up at the terrace. And saw Stone standing there, almost in the same spot and in the same way in which she'd found him.

It was as if he'd never moved.

As if she'd never been there in his arms at all.

Chapter Five

"So what have you decided?"

Ana handed Tara a second cup of coffee, then sat down for a minute to catch her breath. The Sunday afternoon brunch crowd had packed into the restaurant just after church, and today had been Ana's one Sunday to work. Ana had insisted when they opened, that she wouldn't make her staff work every Sunday, so they all rotated, allowing for each of them to have a couple of Sundays a month off to be with their families. She'd also insisted that they didn't open during church hours, so that meant rushing to the restaurant just after Rock's sermon to get things in gear. Tara had to wonder if Ana adhered to her own rule, though. Her sister always seemed to be here in the kitchen, day and night.

"I haven't decided," Tara replied in answer to Ana's question. "There's nothing to decide. And I'm leaving today, anyway. I have to remind myself my life is back in Savannah."

"You're not telling me everything, are you?" Ana asked, pushing a plate of sweet corn muffins and mixed fruit across the counter to her sister. "Eat. You helped serve, so now have some lunch."

Tara picked up a piece of cantaloupe, nibbled on it, then put it back on the plate. Glancing around to make sure none of the staff was nearby, she said, "My life is a mess."

Ana's green eyes widened. "You're still grieving. It's not even a year yet, Tara."

Tara nodded. "Yes, but it's more than just dealing with Chad's death."

"Can you tell me?" Ana asked, her expression full of sisterly concern. "Look, I know you've been confiding in Rock—that's part of his job as a minister— but I'm your sister. Didn't we agree to never again keep any secrets from each other?"

Tara lowered her head, her appetite gone. "Yes. And I do need someone to talk to, another woman."

Ana nodded, let out a sigh. "Even my adorable husband, as sweet and understanding as he is, can't seem to be impartial when it comes to his brother Stone. But I'll try to be, for your sake."

"Why do they hate each other?" Tara asked, memories of Stone's bitter comments about Rock coming to the surface.

"I don't think they hate each other," Ana replied, getting up to stack dishes and put away food. "They're brothers with an eccentric, artist mother who became a widow at a very young age." She gave Tara an apologetic look. "As you know from personal experience, that complicates things right from the start. They resent each other, but you know something I've noticed? Even when Rock is lamenting Stone's transgressions, he still seems to hold a certain amount of respect for Stone's accomplishments.''

"The same with Stone, regarding Rock," Tara said, amazement coloring the realization. "Respect—that's what Stone told me. He wanted to earn my respect.''

Ana sat back down, then picked up a tiny muffin. "Respect is hard to come by. Stone has become very successful, but his motives aren't always so pure, according to what Rock has told me. I think Rock just wants his brother to be happy, and when I say that, I mean happy in his faith, in finding love, in life in general. Stone, for all his riches, seems like a very miserable, lonely man.''

Tara tilted her head. "Is that why you wanted to fix us up? Misery loves company?''

Ana shrugged, bit into her muffin. After chewing a while, she said, "At first, I just thought you two could share companionship, go out together, have some fun. Now, I'm beginning to doubt the wisdom of that particular suggestion. Stone has the power to hurt you, Tara, and I'd never want that.''

Tara knew that to be the truth. Stone did have the power to hurt her, but then last night, he had seemed so alone, so vulnerable. As if he were the one who could be easily hurt.

Ana leaned forward to wave a hand in her face. "Hello? Where'd you just go?''

Tara put her elbows on the counter, then laid her head in her hands. "I'm confused about Stone. He's not the hardened man everyone makes him out to be."

"Hmmm." Ana leaned back in her chair, her eyes centered on her sister. "Are you falling for him, already?"

"No," Tara said, jumping up to busy herself with putting away silverware. "I don't even know him. But he just seems so…lost."

"He is lost," Ana said. "He's lost in that big old mansion. He's lost in a world of greed and money. Rock worries about… Well, he worries about Stone's soul."

"He does have one," Tara said, too defensively.

"Of course he does, but you're not willing to do business with the man, so there must be something about him that scares you."

"There's a lot about Stone Dempsey that scares me, but none of it has to do with business."

"I see." Ana remained quiet for about two seconds. "You are interested in Stone, in more than a business way, aren't you? And that scares you, right?"

Tara nodded. "He kissed me last night."

"Uh-oh. He works fast." Ana came around the counter to stare at Tara. "That is definitely more than business."

"And he offered me a job—he'd still get my land, but he'd hire me on as a partner and pay me a very large salary to be the spokesperson for this new development. I'd deal with selling the acreage to clients, then help them with designing and building their houses to meet the specifications of the overall requirements. Stone plans to build a very exclusive, upscale residential area and a ritzy shopping center. Almost like a private town—a country club behind closed gates.''

Ana stood back, letting what Tara had just told her sink in. ''He's got it all figured out, hasn't he? He gets the land and you—a package deal. No wonder you refused his offer.''

''I can't accept it,'' Tara said. ''Plus, he's offering me this enormous signing bonus. It's just charity, plain and simple. Stone feels sorry for me.''

Ana's head came up. ''And why would he feel sorry for you? You're successful yourself. You've got a nice house in Savannah and a good job. Plus, the assets Chad left you—'' She stopped, her brow lifting. ''Is there more to this, Tara?''

''Chad didn't leave me any assets,'' Tara blurted out, glad to have her horrible secret out in the open. ''He left me a little bit of life insurance and a tremendous amount of debt. And…Stone knows exactly how much I owe. Chad even owed Stone money— that's how Stone got wind of the land being up for sale.''

''What?'' Ana sank down on a counter stool, shock registering on her face. ''But I thought—''

''I didn't want to tell you,'' Tara explained. ''I didn't want you to worry.''

''How bad is it?''

''Pretty bad. I used the life insurance money to pay off the worst of the debts. I'm barely holding on to the house in Savannah. And I don't have anything set aside for the girls' college fund.'' She lowered her head again. "I can barely buy them school clothes. Plus, things are bad at work. There's talk of layoffs. And since that deal near Atlanta fell through, I'll probably be one of the first to go. My boss wasn't too happy that I didn't stay on top of that this summer."

"You were spending time with your children," Ana said. "Did you tell your boss that?"

"Oh, he knew. I tried to explain things to him, but he didn't care." Tara shook her head. "It gets tough out there sometimes."

"I know," Ana replied, sympathy in her eyes. "But Tara, you insisted on loaning me money to start the tea room. How could you do that?"

"It's okay," Tara replied. "That was money already set aside before Chad died. Somehow, he managed one last noble act. He secured the loan for your tea room."

"Oh, my." Ana pushed at her hair. "I can't believe this. There is so much about Chad and you I never knew. First you tell me your marriage was a sham—that Chad still loved me. Now you tell me that your whole lifestyle was a sham, too."

"I told you I was a mess," Tara replied, the words a whisper. "But I don't want my girls to suffer because of my mistakes."

Ana gave her a long, penetrating look. "Maybe you should consider Stone's offer."

"I can't."

"Why? It's a good offer. And it would solve a lot of problems."

"But it could create even more. Think about Rock, Ana."

"I am thinking of Rock. Maybe it's time to put the past behind us. We're doing that, by being honest with each other. Don't you think Stone and Rock need to do that, too?"

"But how can my working for Stone help that?"

"You said he seemed lost," Ana pointed out. "Maybe Stone needs someone like you in his life."

"I'm as lost and miserable as he is. You said so yourself."

"I never said that," Ana replied, shaking her head. "And besides, you've made great strides in your life, and you've done it in spite of all your financial troubles."

Tara bobbed her head, pivoted around the kitchen. "Yes, exactly. Which is why I don't need to be the one to save Stone. I'm having enough trouble just trying to save myself."

"You can't hold out forever," Ana said. "How are you going to pay off the debts?"

"I'm working on finding another buyer for the land."

"But Stone's deal is a good compromise."

Tara finished taking dishes to the big industrial-size dishwasher. "Ana, I've learned a lot about myself over these last few months. Chad kept secrets from me. He was ruthless and he worked all the time—day and night. So did I. I lost him and I've come close to losing my children. Laurel barely speaks to me and Marybeth and Amanda go around dazed and confused. I won't give in to the whims of another powerful man. I can't do it. I'll just have to come up with something else, some other way.''

"You could work here part-time, if that would help,'' Ana suggested. "Just weekends. I'll pay you what I can. A salary coupled with the money I've been paying you back for the loan might help some.''

"That's a nice offer, but how would that help with me spending time with my girls?'' Tara asked, her gaze moving over the oaks and pines outside in the sloping backyard.

"Well, the girls love it here, so they could come with you.''

"No, we won't pile in here on you and Rock every weekend. You're still newlyweds.''

"You can stay in Rock's cottage,'' Ana said, clasping her hands together. "It's vacant now that he's living here. And Milly McPherson would love to have you as a neighbor. Think what a great influence she'd be on the girls.''

Tara stood there thinking it through. "Well, if I do sell the house in Savannah, I'll need a place to stay—but until then, it'd just be for weekends. Of course, I'd have to drive back and forth into the city to work each day, if I did decide to rent the cottage full-time. And Ana, I do mean rent. I won't stay there without paying Rock something.''

"But that would cancel out most of your salary,'' Ana said. "Tara, let us help you. You helped me when I wanted to buy this place. Don't be so stubborn.''

Tara saw the determination in Ana's eyes. "You're right, of course. It would be silly to turn around and pay you back money I need for other things." She held up a hand. "But I'm only going to use the cottage on a temporary basis—just until I can do something about my finances."

"Fine. I'll talk to Rock tonight. Once you get back on your feet, you can make a donation to the church to show your gratitude."

Tara smiled. "This might work. I can use the extra money and the girls will love coming out to the island each weekend. And since I've always set my own hours at the real estate office, I can probably get out here early on Fridays to help you with the occasional dinner crowd, too."

"That would be great. Jackie will be thrilled. She says you know how to sell the artwork better than she does, anyway."

"I do enjoy that," Tara replied, feeling as if a weight had been lifted off her shoulders.

"Of course," Ana said, "I can't pay you nearly what Stone Dempsey is offering."

"No, but you're giving me something much more important than money," Tara said, reaching out a hand to her sister. "You're giving me a chance to redeem myself and help my girls out, too."

Ana laughed. "Now why is that so very different from what Stone was offering you?"

"The difference is," Tara replied, "I can trust you."

"And you'll be safe here," Ana said, her eyes glowing. "Plus, you just might run into Stone here and there, since he'll be staying on the island a while.

You might even get him to come to dinner, or better yet, to church one Sunday."

Tara glared at her sister in astonishment. "Ana Dempsey, did you just set me up?"

"I'm only trying to help," Ana said, grinning.

"And I thought I could trust you." Tara grinned, too, then hugged her sister close. "You're every bit as ruthless as Rock's handsome brother."

"Don't tell Rock," Ana whispered. "He thinks I'm perfect."

Stone glanced up from where he'd been scrubbing down the weathered walls on the west side of the mansion, to find his brother Rock headed toward him. "Perfect. Just perfect."

"Good to see you, too," Rock said as he came up one side of the double-sided stone staircase leading from the pool house and gardens. "I thought you hired people to do the grunt work around here."

"It's Sunday," Stone countered, taking time to wipe sweat from his face with an old towel. "The workers have the day off and I needed some time alone, to think."

"Meaning I should leave?"

Stone turned back to the wall. "Suit yourself."

Rock picked up a long-handled scrub brush and dipped it into the big bucket of bleach and detergent sitting next to Stone's workspace. "Mind if I help?"

"Suit yourself," Stone said again. "But don't you have a sermon to preach or something?"

"Already did that this morning," Rock replied before he pushed the wet broom up against the glinting gray-washed stucco wall. "You might try coming to church sometime."

Stone tore at some clinging ivy with his gloved hands. "I'll pass. You preached to me enough growing up, or have you forgotten?" He heard the tinge of broom brush against aged brick and mortar walls. Apparently, he'd struck a familiar cord.

"I remember," Rock replied, the effort of his work causing him to sound winded. "And obviously, it didn't work. Maybe you should turn to a higher source."

Stone threw down his own scrub brush then turned to face his brother. "What do you want, Rock?"

Rock stopped scrubbing, too. But he held his broom handle near his chest as he stared over at Stone. "Now, that's the question I need to ask you, brother. What exactly do you want from Tara Parnell?"

"Oh, I get it. This is a fact-finding mission," Stone retorted, disgust and frustration causing him to rip away a particularly stubborn vine. Turning to look for his water bottle, he took a long swig, then grudgingly handed it toward Rock. "Thirsty?"

"Thanks." Rock took the water, sipped it, then put it down on a nearby work table. "I don't mean to pry, Stone. But Tara is a nice woman. And she's been through a lot lately."

"Meaning, she doesn't need me complicating her life?"

"Meaning, she doesn't need you in her life, period."

His brother's automatic condemnation rankled

Stone beyond measure, but he hid his discontent behind a blank wall of indifference. "Would I be so bad for Tara? I'm offering her a way out of her situation."

"Are you?" Rock said, leaning back against a granite banister to stare over at Stone. "She didn't really explain your revised contract to any of us."

Stone plopped down on a wide step of the ladder he'd been using to climb up and tear away vines and bushes. "Maybe that's because this is just between Tara and me."

"That's true," Rock said, nodding. "I don't need to know the details, but whatever you offered sure upset her the other night."

Stone felt the weight of a thousand burdens on his back, much like this sinking old house. He'd rather spit nails than ask his brother for advice, but he was becoming desperate. He didn't like that feeling. "I don't want to upset Tara. And I didn't come back here to make trouble for you and Ana. So here's the deal— Tara thinks I'm offering her charity."

"Are you?" Rock asked, all his animosity gone.

Stone looked out over the dense foliage of the overgrown gardens. Tall palms trees and lush wild ferns swayed in the afternoon wind. "I thought I was offering her a solution to all her problems. I don't know how much Tara has told you, but she's not doing so well financially."

"I know," Rock admitted. "She's come to me for counseling."

Stone took that as a given, even though it got to him in more ways than one. He wanted to be the one Tara came to for help, for a shoulder to cry on. He still didn't know or understand why, but his competitive nature told him he didn't like his brother consoling Tara Parnell. Not one bit. So he took up the indifferent attitude again.

"What do you suggest, preacher?"

Rock gave him a long, hard look, then said, "I suggest you back off. Give Tara some space and give her the price she needs for that land so she can get on with her life."

But that would mean he'd also have to let her go, out of his life. And Stone wasn't ready to do that.

"Hey, man, I just saw this as a sound business deal. That land is prime for development, and I've offered a reasonable price. Plus, I've offered Tara a good job that I happen to know she's qualified to handle. She needs to get away from that rinky-dink real estate office and use her talents to make some real money for a change."

Rock pushed off the banister, his face marred with a frown. "It always goes back to money with you, doesn't it?"

Here it comes, Stone thought. The famous Rock Dempsey lecture. "I like money, yeah. And I've got lots of it now. What's wrong with wanting to help someone else make it?"

Rock picked up his scrub brush again. "There is more to life—"

"I know, I know," Stone interrupted, turning to get back to work himself. "There is more to life than money. You've told me that since the day our daddy died." He turned to stare over at Rock. "But you know what, when you don't have money, it becomes the most important thing in the world. And when you do have it—''

''You still can't buy happiness,'' Rock finished for him.

''I'm happy,'' Stone said to hide the hurt he felt rising up inside him like a fast-crashing tide. Throwing his hands out in the air, he added, ''Look around, Rock. Look at what I've accumulated. Why shouldn't I be happy?''

Rock did look around, at the overgrown garden, at the empty, cracked swimming pool covered with water lilies and morning glory vines. At the rose-encroached fountain that no longer flowed with clear, clean water, at the ivy and kudzu threatening to overtake the whole·estate. A cherub with a broken wing looked down on the dry fountain, as if waiting for someone to bring the water back. ''I see what you've accomplished, Stone. And I am proud of you for persevering. But I feel sorry for you, too. 'Thy own reproach alone do fear.'''

Stone let out a groan that echoed over the trees. His brother, ever the philosopher. ''Don't go quoting things to me, Rock. You know that drives me crazy.''

''That quote was on the wall of Andrew Carnegie's private library. Can't remember which house, but it was one of his many castles.''

Stone watched as his brother's gaze traveled over the old mansion. ''Well, obviously I'm not Andrew Carnegie.''

''No, he did good things with his vast fortune. Built libraries and set up foundations.''

Stone put his hands on his hips. "How do you know I'm not doing good things?"

"I truly hope you are, Stone. And I'm not judging you. I actually came here today to offer you my help, with this house, with anything else. No strings attached. That's what the quote means—I think you worry so much about failure, that you're your own worst critic."

Surprised, Stone decided maybe Ana was good for his brother. Maybe being happily married had some merit after all. "Hey, don't go soft on me, brother. *You've* always been my worst critic, remember? But I don't need your sympathy or your constant reminders of my shortcomings. I told you, I'm doing just fine. I don't need your help."

Rock slowly put down his brush, then turned to stare up at Stone, his blue eyes full of regret. "Yeah, I can see that."

"You don't see anything," Stone called after his brother's retreating back. "You just don't get it, Rock."

Rock turned on the weed-infested walkway. "No, you're the one who doesn't get it, brother. But I pray that you will one day, before it's too late."

Angry and defensive, Stone shouted after Rock. "Don't waste your prayers on me. I learned a long time ago that praying doesn't work."

Rock didn't answer him.

But then Stone hadn't expected an answer.

From either his brother or God.

Chapter Six

"You have a knack for selling my work."

Tara looked up from the handful of cash register receipts she'd been sorting to find Eloise Dempsey smiling over at her. "Well, hello. It's very easy to sell your art, Mrs. Dempsey. Your pieces are exquisite."

"Call me Eloise," Stone's mother replied, her cup of hot tea in one hand. "And you're very kind to say that."

"I'm not just being kind," Tara said as she came around the counter and waved to some departing lunch guests. "Having your pieces in the tea room has been a major coup for Ana. Just about half the profits come from the artwork alone, most of that yours. In fact, I just sold that bronze brown pelican to a woman from New York."

"How lovely. I guess they don't see many pelicans in the city."

"I wouldn't think so. She said she'd heard about your sculptures through a friend from Atlanta. Word is getting out about you."

"Well, don't underestimate the other artists around here," Eloise said as she settled back on a wicker chair in a corner, just underneath a Victorian birdhouse. "The art council meets once a month. You should come to a meeting. We could use some fresh, young ideas."

"I'd like that," Tara said, pushing at her bangs. "But as you can see, I'm pretty busy holding down two jobs now."

Eloise nodded, then smiled. "Yes, Ana told me you're helping her out for a while. Splendid idea. And we love having the girls around. That Marybeth, what a doll. Did you know she has a talent for drawing and painting?"

Glancing around to make sure no customers were waiting at the antique counter, Tara sank down on a bistro chair. "No, I didn't. I mean, she's always doodled and colored, but my Marybeth—an artist?"

"She shows tremendous potential," Eloise replied, obviously delighted. "And Amanda wants to learn to play the guitar. I had an old one of Clay's lying about, so I let her fiddle with it. She has a natural ear for music."

Tara didn't know what to say. "Can you explain Laurel to me?"

"Oh, that one." Eloise's hand fluttered out. "Laurel is growing up. She reads a lot. I think she likes to scribble poetry now and again. I've seen her sharing it with that adorable Cal Ashworth."

Tara lowered her head. "I didn't know that. How can I not know these things?"

"Daughters don't always confide in their mothers," Eloise said, taking a sip of her tea. "Nor do sons, for that matter. And speaking of sons, what's going on between you and Stone?"

A bit flustered by Eloise's directness, Tara shrugged. "Nothing. Nothing at all. We came close to agreeing on a business deal, but it stalled out. Your son wants to buy my land, but I can't accept the offer he made."

"Not generous enough?" Eloise questioned, her brilliant silvery eyes, so like Stone's, moving over Tara with a questioning appraisal.

Tara didn't want to go into detail with Stone's mother. "It wasn't that. Stone made me a generous offer, but it had stipulations I couldn't accept."

Eloise sat silent, letting that sink in. "Stone always expects stipulations, I'm afraid. He was a challenge as a child and now he's even harder to deal with as an adult."

"A challenge. Yes, that just about sums him up," Tara replied, glancing at her watch. "Oh, I hate to rush, but I promised the girls we'd go into the city to do some school shopping. And then I think I'll drive them out to the land, let them see the place their father left to us. I don't want to sell it, but I don't know what else to do. I'm sorry you and I can't spend more time talking together."

Eloise waved a hand, her silver bangle bracelets tinkling like chimes as they fell down her arm. "No need to apologize. I'm being nosy, anyway. It's just that Rock and Ana are so happy, and Rock and I are closer than ever. I credit your sister with much of that. She is a gentle force, a good influence on my son. I wish the same for Stone. And he seems smitten with you, dear.''

Tara felt a heat rush up her skin as she remembered Stone's kiss. ''Oh, I think your son is smitten with making more money, with getting the best deal. He seems driven.''

''He is driven. And that's why I pray he'll find someone, the way Rock has, and settle down to the simple pleasures of life.'' She got up, placed a hand on Tara's arm. ''You know, it took me a long time to realize what really matters in this world. You go for that drive with your girls. And while you have them, talk to them. But more important, listen to them. I wish I'd done more of that.'' Then she gave Tara a soft smile. ''Enough unsolicited advice from me. I've got to get home.''

''Work to do?'' Tara asked, still in awe from this entire conversation.

''No,'' Eloise said, running a hand through her short, grayish-white hair. ''I'm going to go for a long walk, maybe over to the other side of the island. To Hidden Hill.''

Tara nodded her understanding. ''To see Stone?''

''He needs me,'' Eloise said. ''I think that's why he's come home. He doesn't realize it, but he has always needed me. And his brothers.''

And me? Tara had to wonder as she waved goodbye to Stone's mother. Then she quickly put that thought out of her mind. And for the last two weeks, she'd tried to put Stone Dempsey out of her mind, too. But it seemed he was always there, the sweet intensity of his touch just a breath away from her dreams.

"Are we all done?" Ana called from the kitchen.

"Yes, thankfully," someone called back.

Tara could hear Jackie and Tina laughing and chatting with Charlotte in the background. Most of the other workers had already gone home for the day. Ana had a wonderful, well-trained staff. They had served a record crowd for lunch and were now shutting down for the day. The Saturday night tourists tended to head to more exciting nightlife than a tea room could offer. But Tara had an idea for something special to draw in people on Saturday night, maybe a nice jazz or classical ensemble playing in the garden.

"What are you dreaming about?" Ana asked from the hallway, jarring Tara out of her musings.

"Oh, just thinking maybe we could hold some Saturday night concerts here, in the garden."

"Hmmm, sure sounds romantic. Girls, what do you think?"

They heard a random groan from the kitchen.

"I'm not sure, but I think that was Charlotte," Ana said with a grin.

"It was Tina," Charlotte called. "We're just too tired right now to think of more work."

Ana leaned into the doorway. "Then go home and soak your feet while my smart sister and I plot more ways to torture you."

"Slave driver," Jackie called as she grabbed her

purse. But she was smiling as she said it. "Anything for you, boss."

"Sure," Ana replied, laughing. "Whew, I'm tired myself. I'm looking forward to a nice quiet evening with my husband." Then she turned to Tara. "What are you going to do for the rest of the afternoon?"

Tara finished closing down the cash register. "I'm going to take the girls for a drive, out to our land. I don't think they've ever been there. Then we might do some shopping in town."

"Do you need any money—for clothes, I mean."

"I'm not that destitute yet," Tara replied, hating the sympathy in Ana's eyes, even if she did appreciate the gesture.

"Okay. Just checking. Is everything all right?"

"I'm hanging on by a thread," Tara admitted. "The extra money I'm making here has helped so much already. And the girls love their new weekend retreat. Even Laurel seems to be having fun." She grinned. "Of course, Milly McPherson is trying to teach them manners. She said they need to learn how to be proper ladies."

Ana laughed. "Did she suggest they wear hats and gloves to church?"

"Yes, I think she did," Tara replied. "Laurel went running in the other direction."

"Well, they do have some manners. They were a big help around the kitchen today," Ana said as she took off her ruffled apron and hung it on a peg by the back door. "They're good girls, Tara."

"I know. And Rock is such a sweetheart to take

them off my hands for a while this afternoon. That poor man must think he's a built-in baby-sitter.''

"Hush, he loves being with the girls. And teaching them to fish—he couldn't be any happier on a pretty Saturday afternoon.''

Tara nodded. ''Well, I'd better go down to the dock and gather them up. Maybe we'll have fish for supper, huh?''

"Maybe.'' Ana waited for Tara to gather her tote bag before letting her out the back. ''Have you heard anything else from Stone?''

"Not to change the subject,'' Tara replied, her smile teasing. ''No, I haven't heard anything else from Stone and if I get another offer on the land, I'm taking it. I can't hold out forever.''

"You could just accept his offer, stipulations and all.''

"Trying to get rid of me already?''

"No, not at all. I love having you help out around here. You've freed up the wait staff to concentrate on the food and you're very good at persuading the customers to buy our artwork. I just… Well, Rock has always indicated that Stone is selfish and hostile. I just wonder why Stone would make you such a strange and generous offer. Maybe you should talk to him about it a little more.''

"Are you still trying to fix me up with Rock's brother?''

"Maybe,'' Ana admitted as they strolled down the steps toward the dock at the end of the property.

"You don't think I'm selfish and hostile, do you?''

"No,'' Ana said, taking in a deep breath of the

fresh tropical air. "And honestly, I don't believe Stone is any of those things, either. Rock just worries about him. I don't know why, but my instincts tell me you and Stone would be right for each other."

"Your instincts also told you to break up with Chad way back in college, so he could be with me, remember?"

Ana cringed. "Okay, point taken. I'll try to stay out of it."

Tara touched a hand to her sister's arm. "I appreciate your trying to find me a new man, Ana. But I'm not ready for anything serious just yet. I have to get my life straight, first."

"You're right, of course. You've been through a lot. And I need to remember that."

"Thanks for caring," Tara said, meaning it. She and Ana had grown close over the summer, thanks to some heart-to-heart talks and Rock's gentle urgings that Tara and the girls get involved in church.

Having Ana and Rock to confide in had helped Tara deal with Chad's death and the fact that their marriage had been in shambles long before he died. As Tara saw her girls laughing and talking to Rock, she couldn't help but think of all they were missing, not having a father to love them. Chad had loved his daughters. That much, at least, Tara knew to be true.

That made her think of Rock and Stone, and their brother Clay. They'd had to grow up without a father, too. Rock had been the oldest, the one who had to stay strong for everyone else. He'd carried the weight of the entire family on his shoulders. Stone was the middle child. The one who got lost in the shuffle of the bossy firstborn and the sweet, lovable baby brother, Clay. No wonder Stone had a chip on his shoulder. He'd probably never felt truly loved, even though it was obvious Eloise loved each of her sons equally.

But how did a parent prove that love to a child?

How did a parent show that love to a grown man?

I won't feel this way, Tara told herself as she waved to the children and Rock. I won't feel sorry for Stone Dempsey. I won't feel anything.

But each time she remembered his eyes, his touch, his kiss, she felt funny little sensations, starting with a tingling on her skin, then moving to a gentle fluttering inside her stomach, then finally causing a slight acceleration in her heartbeat. Just nerves, she thought. She'd been wise to turn down Stone's offer.

"Mom, I caught a fish!" Marybeth exclaimed, holding up the fishing line to show her mother her prize. "But I'm gonna throw him back. I don't want him to die."

"That's very sweet, honey." Tara whispered to Ana, "Marybeth is my environmentalist. She believes in taking care of Mother Earth."

"A very noble cause," Ana said, smiling over at her husband.

Rock grinned the goofy grin of a man in love. "What brings you two lovely ladies down to the water?"

"I came to collect my children," Tara said, her gaze moving over Marybeth's dark hair and eyes, so much like her aunt Ana's. Laurel and Amanda had the blond hair and blue eyes of Tara and their grandfather, Martin. But Marybeth looked a lot like Ana and Grandmother Peggy. All of the girls had their father's distinctive characteristics, too—tall, lanky, big toothy smiles.

"My children are so beautiful," Tara said, again under her breath.

"Yes, they are." Ana moved toward the dock, then sank down beside Rock. He gave her a quick peck on the cheek.

"Want to fish?" he asked, offering her the pole, a mischievous look in his blue eyes.

Ana leaned close to nudge his side. "I just might, at that."

Tara took that as a good sign that her sister and brother-in-law wanted to be left alone. "Okay, girls, let's load up. If you want to make it to the mall before it closes, we'd better hurry."

"I need new shoes," Laurel said, her sulkiness just a tad above tolerant.

"And I need some jeans and shirts," Marybeth explained, tossing her bobbed hair off her face.

Tara sighed, then turned to Amanda. "What do you need?"

"I'm fine," Amanda said, her big eyes on her mother. "I can wear whatever doesn't fit Laurel."

"Don't be silly," Tara said, frowning. "You can get some new things, too."

Amanda shifted on her feet, digging her sneakers into the planks of the weathered dock. "But…I don't want you to have to spend extra money on me."

Tara glanced over to Rock and Ana. Her sister shot her a sympathetic look. "Honey, I have some extra cash, thanks to working for Aunt Ana. We'll be fine. You can buy a few things, too, okay?''

"Okay," Amanda said, smiling at last. "If you're sure."

"I am sure," Tara replied, not really sure at all. But she'd make do. She had a closet full of designer clothes she could wear for many years to come. Her children were growing, though. They needed new clothes. She had enough money tucked back to buy them a couple of outfits each, at least.

"We're going," she said to Ana. "We're just going to stay in town tonight, since it'll be late when we leave the mall. So I guess I'll see you again next weekend."

"Okay," Ana said as she baited a hook with a squirming worm. "Thanks for the help yesterday and today."

Amanda ran over to Ana and Rock, her arms going around both of them. "Thank you, Aunt Ana, for paying us a salary, too."

"Shhh," Ana said, her gaze catching Tara's. "You weren't supposed to tell." She shrugged, a sheepish look on her face as she looked up at Tara. "I gave them each a tip. They worked hard, so that's fair."

Tara shook her head and mouthed her own thanks. Her sister had come through for her, even after all these years, even after the way things had turned out in college when Tara had practically stolen Ana's boyfriend Chad Parnell away from her.

Somehow, Tara would repay Ana and Rock for their kindness. Somehow.

It occurred to her that if she took Stone up on his

offer, she'd have the money to do that and more. Maybe it was time to put pride and personal feelings aside, for the sake of her children.

Stone stood on a high bluff overlooking the land he hoped to buy from Tara Parnell. To the north, the Savannah River glistened and flowed off in the distance, headed toward the outer banks and on to the Atlantic Ocean. To the south, a vast forest and marshland grew up around a small freshwater lake. White ibis birds strolled in the reeds and bushes on the salt marsh, while overhead a flight of brown pelicans moved in perfect symmetry out toward the sea.

Stone stood and waited.

His mother had told him Tara would be coming here today. Since Stone believed in available opportunities instead of destiny or coincidences, he'd talked politely to his mother and bided his time until he could drive the hour or so to get here.

And wait.

He wanted to talk to Tara again. About the land, about the plans he had, about her working for him to make those plans happen, about him and her and where they might be headed. Stone had lots to discuss with Tara Parnell. And he wasn't leaving until she listened to him.

It was time to put everything out on the table. Time to make one last play for the intriguing woman he couldn't seem to get out of his mind.

So he stood, listening, waiting, anticipating.

Stone heard a movement to his left and turned to find an old black man walking toward him. The man wore a battered straw hat and overalls. He walked with the help of a huge carved walking stick. Stone stared at the man, wondering where in the world he'd come from. This land was empty, vast, hidden away from the world.

"Hello, young fellow," the old man said, waving a withered hand in greeting. "Nice day for a walk, ain't it?"

"Uh, yes," Stone replied, once again glancing around to look for another car back on the sandy dirt lane. But Stone only saw his own sturdy SUV. "Do you live around here?" he asked the old man.

The man stopped to catch his breath, then leaned heavily on his walking stick. Slowly, he took off his hat and shook it out in his hand. His face was wrinkled and wizened, like a raisin dried by the sun. His hair was completely white and tightly curled. It sat against his rounded head like cotton tufts falling away from a brown bale. But his eyes, they held Stone's attention.

The man had old eyes, big and black and all-seeing, in spite of the watery age spots clouding his pupils. Those eyes seemed to see right through Stone's soul.

Finally, the man answered. "I live back there in the marsh," he explained, indicating with a thumb over his shoulder. "Near the chapel."

"Chapel? What chapel?" Again, surprise caused Stone to glance around.

"It doesn't really have a name," the man said, his grin revealing a gold tooth right in the front of his mouth. "We've just always called it the chapel. It's been here since the beginning."

"The beginning?"

"When the first slaves came over," the man said, no censure or condemnation, just acceptance, in his rich baritone voice. "They built it right there between the marsh and the sand dunes. It only holds about twenty people. But it's still a house of God."

Fascinated, Stone asked, "And this chapel is still standing? It must be over two hundred years old, at least."

"At least," the man repeated, grinning again. "Would you like to see the place?"

Stone glanced at his watch. What if he missed Tara?

"In a hurry to get somewhere?" the old man asked.

"No. Just...I was planning on meeting someone here. But I'm probably early anyway."

"Is this someone important to you?"

"You could say that."

"A woman, maybe?"

"How could you know that?"

"Son, it's written all over your face," the old man said. "And me, I can see things. Signs of things to come."

"Oh, really." Stone doubted that. Maybe he should just leave. And yet, something told him to stay. "Who are you, anyway?"

"Samson Josiah Bennett," the man proudly said, extending a gnarled hand toward Stone. "I'm the preacher."

"At the chapel?" Stone asked, thinking this was getting more strange by the minute.

"Yep. Call me Josiah. Everybody does."

Again, Stone nodded. "And Josiah…you live on this land?"

"Lived here since the day I was born. Most folks have moved away, but I stayed. Married in the chapel, raised a family right here, but now it's just me. I like the peace and quiet of the marsh."

"And you preach in the chapel each Sunday?"

"Yep. Sometimes, I get two or three people. Sometimes, I just sit and talk to the Lord."

"I see." Stone was beginning to wonder if he'd stumbled across an escaped nursing home dweller.

"Do you want to see my church, or not?" Josiah asked, still leaning on his walking stick.

"Are you sure you're okay?" Stone moved toward the man. In spite of being old, he looked in pretty good health.

"I'm fine, just fine," Josiah said. "I don't get many visitors, is all. When I heard your vehicle pulling up, I came to investigate."

"You know this land is up for sale, don't you?" Stone asked as he strolled along to accommodate the man's snail pace.

"Yep."

"Where will you go if someone buys the land?"

Josiah chuckled, waved a hand in the air. "That's for the Lord to decide, I reckon."

Stone shook his head. "I don't depend on the Lord in life. I make my own way." And he didn't usually discuss religion with strangers.

"Do you now?" Josiah said, bobbing his head like an old turtle.

Stone glanced back toward the empty land. Where was Tara?

"She'll wait for you," Josiah said, as if reading Stone's mind.

"It's a business deal," Stone felt obligated to explain. "I might buy this land."

"I figured as much," Josiah replied, his face perfectly serene in spite of the wrinkle traces dragging his skin down.

Stone wanted it understood. "You'd have to leave."

"Maybe. Or maybe you'd let me stay."

Oh, great. Not only was he dealing with a stubborn, beautiful woman, but now Stone had to try to persuade this ancient preacher to pack up and move. "You wouldn't be able to stay," he tried to explain. "We'd be putting in a new development."

"I see new development out here in these woods and marshes every single day, son."

"I don't understand," Stone replied, perplexed.

"I know you don't," Josiah conceded. "That's why you need to visit my chapel."

Chapter Seven

"I don't get why we have to come out here," Laurel said as Tara turned her car up the dirt lane toward the property. "This is so lame."

"I told you, I wanted you to see this place," Tara replied, tired of explaining herself.

"But the mall will close," Laurel whined, her arms crossed in a rebellious tightening over her midsection.

Tara glanced across at her daughter. "The mall stays open until ten o'clock, Laurel."

"I want to see the land, Mom," Amanda said, leaning over the seat to stare ahead. "Wow, this is sure out in the country."

Marybeth leaned forward, too. "It's so pretty."

"It's hot and full of bugs, and probably lots of snakes, too," Laurel told her sisters with a tart tongue. "You two are such losers."

"Hush," Tara said, glaring at Laurel. "You will not speak to your sisters that way."

"Well, it's true," Laurel said, raising her voice. "We're all losers. You think we don't see, Mom. But we do. You're working now more than ever, when you promised you were going to spend more time with us. We can't even buy decent clothes for school. And all my friends keep asking why our house is up for sale."

"Laurel, that is enough," Tara said, bringing the car to such a fast halt, the tires skidded on the sandy dirt. "I am doing the best I can. And I am spending time with you. That's why I brought you here."

"Just so we could see this?" Laurel asked, her hand on the door handle. "Just so you could tell us how much our daddy loved us, then turn around and sell the land he left us? That makes perfect sense, Mom."

Tara sat with her hands on the steering wheel, clutching it as if it were a life preserver. Her two younger daughters had now slumped into their seats, their eyes wide, their faces devoid of any smiles.

She wouldn't break down. She couldn't do that in front of her children. She'd gotten them into this mess, and she'd have to be the one to get them out now that Chad was gone. "I'm sorry," she said, the whispered apology laced with a plea. "Things are going to get better, I promise."

"We don't believe your promises," Laurel said. Then she got out of the car and slammed the door.

"I believe you, Mommy," Amanda said, her voice sounding small and far away.

"Me, too," Marybeth chimed in. "Laurel is so weird. Don't listen to her, Mom."

Tara swiped a tear from her face. "Thanks for the support, you two. Do you want to do this? We could just go on to the mall."

"I want to see this place," Marybeth replied, her eyes capturing Tara's in the rearview mirror. "If Daddy loved it, then we will, too."

That simple declaration almost broke Tara's heart, but she regained control and got out of the car. That's when she spotted the sleek black SUV parked off the road, underneath an aged live oak.

The girls got out, too. "Who's here, Mom?" Amanda asked, glancing over at the SUV.

"I don't know," Tara said. "I haven't had any calls from prospective buyers, so I wasn't supposed to meet anyone out here."

"Maybe somebody saw your ad in the paper," Marybeth reasoned. "They might have just decided to look on their own."

"That could be it," Tara replied, careful to glance around. They were in a very remote location. She wouldn't want any harm to come to her daughters.

They walked up on the slight incline that allowed a view of the marsh and forest. This was the spot where Chad had always talked about building a cabin or cottage. Tara turned to Laurel to tell her that, but the teenager hung back, her face sullen, her whole body rigid with anger and pain.

Tara wanted to run to her daughter and take Laurel into her arms and tell her it would be okay, but she didn't do that. Instead, she just stood looking out over the quiet marshland.

Then she heard laughter and voices coming from

the lane that followed the course of the river to one side and stayed high above the marsh to the other. "I guess we do have visitors, girls."

Tara waited to see who would emerge from the woods around the bend. And wondered if she really did want to sell this land after all.

He had to wonder now if he should even buy this land.

Stone stared over at the intriguing man who'd taken him on a journey that had revealed more than just the marsh and a tiny ancient chapel.

The chapel was amazing. It looked like a little dollhouse, sitting among the old live oaks and cypress trees. It was painted a bright white with red shutters and a matching red door. A crudely made cypress cross was centered over the door. Inside, the chapel was quiet and cool, the scent of vanilla candles long since burned down wafting out into the small aisle. Josiah had invited Stone to sit up front, close to the petite altar, but Stone had hung back while Josiah piddled with clearing away cobwebs and dusting off the pulpit.

And Josiah had not bothered him.

Stone had sat inside that little clapboard building, in the peace and quiet that had endured through slavery and a great war, and somehow, had touched on the shackles and wars of his very own soul. And to think, no one believed he actually had a soul.

But Josiah had seen inside his soul.

Coincidence? Or an opportunity? An opportunity for what, Stone thought now as he strolled along, listening to Josiah's aged Southern drawl. There couldn't be any opportunity in taking a man from his home. Stone was accustomed to corporate raiding, but he'd never intentionally raid the home of someone so innocent and centered, so grounded in a simple way of life.

Stone decided he wouldn't worry about that until he'd signed on the dotted line. He'd make sure Josiah got to a safe, nice new home. He'd also make sure the old preacher wanted for nothing, ever again.

But Josiah seemed to have everything he needed right here, a little voice nagged in Stone's head. The old man had his chapel and he had his tiny, gray-washed shack that sat precariously close to the marsh. Josiah lived mostly off the land and the kindness of the few who still came to hear him preach the gospel each Sunday.

Wouldn't the old man be better off somewhere safe and warm, Stone wondered. Josiah whistled as they walked, making Stone think that maybe the old man would never willingly leave the marsh.

For the first time, Stone had doubts about his grand plans.

Then he looked up to the bluff and saw Tara standing there with her three daughters. The wind was playing through Tara's hair as she held her arms on one of the girl's shoulders. She looked down at him, their eyes locking, and Stone felt something break loose inside his very being, as if a strong wall had cracked open to reveal the secret places of his heart. And suddenly, he felt as if he were the one without a place to call home.

"Is that her?" Josiah asked, the words falling across the wind like a butterfly's flutter.

"Yes." Stone couldn't take his eyes off her.

"She's a pretty little thing."

"Yes," he repeated, sounding stupid and redundant in his own mind.

"Got a family already, too."

"Yes," he said again. "She's a widow."

"I know who she is," Josiah replied just before they reached the copse of trees on the bluff. "That's Chad Parnell's widow."

"You knew Chad?" Stone asked, completely surprised by this new information. But then, this day had been full of surprises.

"Known him since he was a boy," Josiah said. "Chad used to come out here…a lot. He'd fish and hunt with his daddy. He'd come to my chapel, too."

"Chad Parnell attended church?"

"He didn't attend church, son. He came to talk to a friend about all his troubles."

"And you listened and gave him advice?"

Josiah chuckled and shook his head. "No, young fellow, *God* listened…and gave him solace."

Stone turned to face Josiah at last. "I didn't think Chad Parnell was a godly man."

"Did you ever think to ask him?" Josiah shot back.

"Well, no. I mean, I didn't know him that well."

"Some things are kept close to the heart," Josiah replied. "Chad knew the Lord. He just didn't know how to accept all the Lord's blessings."

"I guess he didn't," Stone replied, his gaze moving back to Tara.

Josiah motioned toward Tara. "You might be able to do a better job than Chad."

Stone wished the old man was right. But the concept was so foreign to him, he didn't even know how to begin to ask for God's blessings. Especially regarding Tara Parnell.

Again, it was if Josiah had read his mind. "Ask and ye shall receive. Knock and He will answer."

Stone knew what Josiah was saying. After all, Rock had often coaxed him to turn his life around by turning back to the God that Stone had abandoned. Or rather, the God that Stone believed had abandoned him and his family.

Suddenly, Stone felt so very tired. Tired of fighting against his brother's constant suggestions and gentle admonishments, tired of fighting against the God he didn't want to accept or acknowledge. And yet, he realized he needed some sort of acceptance, some sort of solace, himself. Meeting Tara had brought out all the loneliness he tried so hard to hide.

"I've been knocking, Josiah. It's like beating my head against a wall." This time, he wasn't just talking about Tara. It seemed as if Stone had been knocking against a brick wall most of his life.

"Then it's time to bring that wall down," Josiah said on a calm voice. "Starting right now, I think."

Stone stared up at Tara. She hadn't moved, hadn't said a word in greeting. Her three girls stood there with her, staring at him as if he were a marsh monster.

He turned to say something to Josiah, but the old man was already walking away.

Which left Stone alone in the middle of the marsh, alone and more confused and afraid than he'd ever been in his life.

She'd never expected to find Stone Dempsey here.

Tara's heart took flight like the big heron the two men had scared away with their conversation.

"What are you doing here?" she asked Stone as he strolled toward them. "And who on earth was that man?"

"Hello to you, too," Stone replied, smiling down at Amanda. "My name is Stone."

"You're Rock's brother," Amanda announced, her eyes going wide as she glanced over her shoulder at her mother.

Stone nodded, grinned. "Yes. What's your name?"

"Amanda." She pointed a finger. "That's Marybeth." Then she rolled her eyes toward Laurel. "And that's Laurel."

"Hello, Amanda, Marybeth and Laurel," Stone said, taking the time to shake each girl's hand, even though Laurel just glared at him. "I saw you at the wedding, but didn't get a chance to speak to any of you. Y'all are just about as pretty as your mom."

Tara had her guard up. This was no coincidence. Stone had obviously planned to find her here. "Hello," she said finally. "Now tell me what you're doing here?"

"I came out to look over this property once again. You know, just biding my time until you make a decision."

"I won't be making any decisions, at least not regarding you," Tara said, careful that she kept her tone very impersonal and businesslike. Laurel was already giving her keen, condemning looks.

Stone stood silent, letting her curt words wash over him. "Did you know about Josiah?"

"Who's that?" Marybeth asked.

"The man I was with," Stone explained. "He came walking up the lane when I first arrived. He has a cabin back in the marsh. And the tiniest little chapel."

Tara was surprised to hear that. "What are you talking about? This land is vacant."

"No, not quite," Stone replied. "Samson Josiah Bennett lives on the edge of this land, near where the river and the marsh merge. Apparently, he's lived here all of his life and your husband knew him."

Tara glanced in the direction the old man had gone. "Are you serious?"

"Very," Stone said. "He kind of took me by surprise, too. Apparently, Chad knew Josiah lived here when he bought the land years ago, but he let Josiah stay. This adds a new wrinkle to things."

"It sure does," Tara agreed. "Why didn't Chad ever mention him?"

Laurel stalked close then. "Maybe because you were never around to talk to Dad."

Tara whirled to her daughter. "Did you know about this man?"

"No," Laurel admitted. "But Dad never talked to us about anything, either." She shrugged and went back into full hostile mode.

"Mom, if you sell the land, that old man will have

to move," Marybeth said, worry clouding her green eyes.

"I know, honey. I'll have to think about what needs to be done."

"Let's think about it together," Stone suggested. "Over dinner."

"I can't," Tara replied, disappointment warring with common sense. "I told the girls we'd go to the mall out on the interstate."

"I'll go with you then."

Tara stood back, baffled by both his tone and the soft warmth in his eyes. That warmth took her breath away more than his cold, icy stares ever could.

And she wondered what had come over the man.

Laurel shuffled in the background, bringing Tara to full alert. "Mom, if we don't hurry, we won't get dinner or shopping. And why does he have to come along?"

"Don't be rude," Tara said on a low warning.

"I won't be too much of a bother," Stone said, giving Laurel a brilliant smile. "And I'm buying. Just name the restaurant."

He got at least two different choices. "Pizza," Amanda shouted, dancing around. "Hamburgers," Marybeth said at the same time.

"How about we go where they have both?" Stone asked, his eyes on Tara again. "Laurel, where do you want to eat?"

"I don't care," Laurel said on a huff of breath. "I'm not even hungry."

"What's your favorite dessert?" Stone asked, stepping so close Laurel had to acknowledge him.

Laurel hesitated, tried to keep the pout on her face, then finally said, "Chocolate pie."

"Okay, then. It's chocolate pie for dessert. I know a great little pie shop right in the heart of Savannah."

"I haven't said we'd go to dinner with you," Tara reminded him, eternally thankful in spite of her qualms that he was being so thoughtful toward her girls.

His silver eyes held her spellbound. "But you will, won't you?"

She thought about it for a minute. They did need to talk, about a lot of things. She had almost convinced herself to give in to his offer, but now they had Josiah Bennett to worry about. And she wanted to know more about Josiah's relationship with Chad.

She turned to the girls. "Do you want Stone to take us to dinner?"

There was a chorus of voices. Two yeses. One no.

"Two out of three isn't bad," Stone quipped, giving Laurel a wink. Then he looked back at Tara. "I didn't hear your vote."

"Okay, we'll go," she said finally. "But only if we can let the girls shop first. If you don't mind?"

"I don't mind one bit," Stone said, his smile sincere and full of hope. "Why don't I follow you to your house and then we'll head to the mall in my vehicle?"

"All right," Tara said, nodding. Then she stopped, "Girls, I'm sorry. I brought you out here to see this land because…well, selling it is your decision, too."

"Funny you never bothered to ask us about that

before,'' Laurel said, tossing her hair as she stomped toward the car.

Tara looked over at Stone, the heat of her shame rushing up her face. "She's right. I never stopped to consider how they would feel."

"Do we have to sell it, Mom?" Marybeth asked, her green eyes moving over the lush marsh. "Look at the birds. Where will they go if you build houses here?"

Stone touched on Marybeth's ponytail. "We'd make sure we leave plenty of trees and bushes for the birds, honey. They'll be safe. We wouldn't touch the marsh. We just want to build houses up on the bluff here."

"Why?" Marybeth asked.

Stone gave Tara a helpless look that caused her to smile in spite of her embarrassment. He obviously hadn't had many dealings with teenaged girls.

"Well," he said, "it's a good investment, for your mom and for my company."

"Mom could use a few good investments," Amanda volunteered. "We're flat broke."

"Amanda!" Tara's felt sweat trickling down her back.

"Well, it's the truth," Amanda replied, her gaze moving from her mom's face to Stone. "But can't you find some other way to make money? I like this place just the way it is."

Stone let out a long breath. "Let's talk more about it over dinner," he suggested as a means of stalling.

"Good idea," Tara said, watching as he walked to his SUV. He looked good in his faded jeans and soft

yellow polo shirt. Too good. She got in the car, turned
it around on the road, then headed toward the high-
way that would take them into Savannah.

"Why are you seeing him?" Laurel asked, her
harsh gaze full of accusation.

Not wanting to get into another argument, Tara
thought about her answer to that question. "I'm not
seeing him. We are conducting a business deal. And
he is Rock's brother, after all, so we'll probably see
him a lot from now on."

"I don't like him," Laurel replied.

"I didn't ask you to like him," Tara countered. "I
only ask that you treat him politely. I did teach you
manners, remember, Laurel."

"He seems nice," Marybeth said from the back
seat.

"How do you know that?" Laurel said over her
shoulder. "You just met the man."

"I saw him at the wedding," Marybeth reminded
her.

"Me, too," Amanda said. "He's handsome."

"Oh, please!" Laurel let out a groan then reached
for her ever constant headphones.

Tara didn't stop her. She had enough to deal with.
Stone was following her home. Chad had kept yet
another secret from her. And her oldest daughter obviously hated the world in general. Wondering when
she'd ever find some peace in her life, Tara sent up
a little prayer for God's guidance. *Show me the way,
Lord. Help me to understand what I'm supposed to
do next.*

Tara felt tired, so tired. She needed some rest, some

solace. And she decided in a fit of defeat, she needed that job Stone had offered her. She'd tell him tonight that she'd sign the contract. He could have the land to develop, and she could finally have some peace of mind.

And together, they'd have to figure out what to do about Josiah Bennett.

Chapter Eight

"What's it like, having three daughters?"

Stone watched Tara's face light up before she answered his question. They were sitting in the food court at the mall, in a spot where Tara could see Marybeth and Amanda looking over clothes in the boutique next door. Laurel had taken off to another store across the way, with strict instructions from Tara to stay close.

"It's a challenge," she said through a soft smile. "It's been hard since Chad died. The girls loved their father."

Stone felt the cut of that declaration down to his bones. He certainly understood that feeling. "And you...you loved Chad? I mean, did you have a good marriage?"

She looked across the table at him, the shock on her face causing her to frown. "Of course I did." Then she lowered her head. "That's not exactly true.

We married soon after we met, mostly on impulse and a physical attraction. Then we drifted apart after the girls were born. We had some problems toward the end—lots of problems. He had become withdrawn, quiet.'' She stopped, took a sip of her soft drink. ''I thought…I thought he regretted marrying me. But looking back, I think he was just worried about our finances. I wish he'd opened up to me about that. But Chad kept it all inside. I think that's probably why he had a heart attack.''

Stone could see the regret and sadness in her blue eyes. She wasn't telling him everything, but then, he didn't expect her to. That was her business. ''You blame yourself, don't you?''

She didn't look up. She just nodded. ''And Laurel blames me, too. She's so angry.''

Stone had to swallow back his own burning anger. ''I know exactly how she feels. I felt the same way when my father died. It's not right, it's not fair, but there it is.''

Tara lifted her head, her gaze locking with his. ''Is that why you aren't close to your family now?''

''I'm not close to anyone,'' he said, the bitterness creeping into his voice in spite of his low tone. ''My father's death has colored my whole outlook on life. I blamed my mother most of all, and Rock, too.'' At least he could admit that now. And only to her, even though Stone knew it was fairly obvious in his family.

''But why?'' Tara asked, her eyes wide with concern and questions. ''Why would you blame them for something that was beyond their control? And why does Laurel blame me?''

"I can't speak for Laurel," Stone said, wondering if he even wanted to go down this road, "but as for me, I blame my mother for her pride. We could have had a better life if she'd only turned back to my grandparents for help. If she had accepted their help, my father might not have been out on that shrimp boat during that hurricane."

"But I thought they disowned her."

"They did at first. But after we all came along, they tried to get involved in our lives again. Our mother refused their overtures of help. Said they'd just try to mold us into what they thought we should be."

Tara gazed at him for a long time, then said, "Ana told me about them. They were wealthy?"

"Yes. They owned homes in Savannah and the house my mom lives in on the island. They disinherited her when she married my father, but as I said, they did offer her money through the years—for the sake of the children, they would tell her—and after his death they tried to make amends. My mother just kept refusing their help. She only accepted the island house, so we'd have a place to live. But it was run-down and old."

He shifted on his seat, his discomfort stifling him. Stone had never talked to anyone about his childhood. But being around Tara was making him see things in a different light. "I remember when the storms would roll in off the Atlantic. My bedroom leaked—a spot right over my bed. I'd have to climb in bed with Rock in his room, just to stay dry and warm. On those nights, I always thought of my father and how much I missed him. Rock tried hard to replace him." He had a flash of memory, a memory of Rock reaching out an arm to him as lightning flared through a window, telling him not to worry, he'd take care of him.

"So you and Rock were close back then?"

He shrugged, let the memory sink back into a veil of bitterness, then settled back on the metal chair. "Yes and no. We fought like most brothers do, but as we got older, something changed. Rock was always the protector. He was the oldest, so he felt like he had to prove something to the rest of us. But he started bossing us around. I resented that, so I did whatever I could to revolt against his authority."

"And you're still doing that?"

He chuckled. "I guess I am."

"What about Clay?"

"Clay is as good as gold. We get along just fine. But I don't see him very much."

"Sounds like he works a lot of long hard hours in Atlanta."

"He's a K-9 cop and Atlanta is a big place."

"I didn't get to talk to him very much at the wedding."

Stone leaned forward then. "Well, maybe you'll get to know him more when he comes home for vacation in a few weeks."

"Will you still be around then?"

"Is that a trick question?"

He waited as she gave him a long, searching look. "Stone, I've been thinking about your proposal."

His heart hammered against his chest. He ignored it. "And?"

"I think I should accept it."

He didn't want to appear too anxious. So he just tapped his fingers against the red metal table. And watched her face. And remembered how soft her lips were.

"That is, if you still want to do this," she said, her eyes flashing with worry and wonder. "Stone?"

He stopped drumming his fingers. "Oh, absolutely. I'm just curious. What made you change your mind?"

Tara glanced up to see her children walking toward the table. "Them," she said on a whisper. "And something you just said. Sometimes we need to swallow our pride for the sake of our children. I need to take care of my girls."

It occurred to Stone as to why he might be trying to help Tara Parnell. It was because as a child he had longed to hear his own mother say those exact same words. He had wanted his mother to care about them. He had wanted her to put aside her pride and her ambition for the sake of her children. But she hadn't done that. And now, she was trying very hard to make amends. Too late, in Stone's book. But he could be civil. He could be courteous and polite. While deep inside, he still longed to hear those words. And he longed to be a real son to a real mother. A real brother to Rock and Clay, not just a polite stranger who wandered in now and again.

If he couldn't do that, he could at least do the next best thing. He could save Tara's children from the same fate. "Your girls will be taken care of," he said, meaning it. "You have my promise on that."

"I don't want charity," she reminded him. "But I'm not as strong-willed as your mother apparently was. I can swallow my pride to help my girls, but I don't want a handout.''

"This isn't charity, Tara. This is a good business move." Then he touched a finger to her hand. "And this is between friends."

"Are we that? Friends?"

"I'd like to think so. But I meant what I said. I want you to respect me, too."

"I believe you. But can I trust you?"

He got up, threw his drink cup in a nearby trash container. "That's up to you, isn't it?"

"I think we need to set a few guidelines," Tara told Stone later that night. "And we've got to decide what to do about Josiah."

They were back at Tara's house in Savannah. The girls had found a few things for school and were now upstairs trying on clothes. Tara could hear them giggling and talking.

Except for Laurel. She'd bought one outfit that had turned out to be much more provocative than Tara normally allowed. They had argued about returning it, so as soon as they'd gotten home, she'd stalked up to her room and slammed the door. Tara could only guess her eldest daughter was now listening to loud music with her headphones.

To shut out the pain, Tara thought.

"Hey, where'd you go?" Stone asked as he handed her a cup of coffee.

Tara glanced around to find him leaning on her kitchen counter. It seemed strange to see another man standing there in the spot where Chad had moved and lived. But it was also comforting. Too comforting.

"I'm just worried about Laurel. She's so lost and confused."

"She's a teenager," Stone reasoned. "Hard to figure out on a good day."

Tara decided to bring the subject back around to business. "That's why it's important that we have an understanding, Stone. If I work for you—"

"When you work for me," he corrected, "you will have control over your time, Tara. Since I know everything—all about your debts, your need to spend time with your children, and that you have the prettiest blue eyes I've ever seen, I think we can work on all the details as we go along."

"But you can't do that," she said, lifting a hand in the air.

"Do what?"

"Tell me I have pretty eyes. Flirt with me. I can't have you hovering about if you're my boss, Stone."

"I'll stay away during business hours, then. Unless, of course, we have business to discuss. Oh, and speaking of that, don't worry about Josiah. I'll make sure he has a safe place to live."

"He might not want to leave."

"I've thought about that. We'll have a Plan B."

"Was he close to Chad? Did he talk about him?"

Stone watched her, as if trying to decide how much of the truth she could handle. "He said Chad had a good heart, but that he didn't know how to appreciate all his blessings."

"That sounds about right. We didn't realize we had so much, and I don't mean material things."

"He also said Chad came to his little chapel to pray and talk to God."

"My Chad? He never attended church. We never had time."

"Apparently, Chad did have a relationship with Christ. At least Josiah implied that."

Tears brimmed in Tara's eyes. "That brings me some comfort at least. I just wish he could have talked to me."

"Stop tormenting yourself," Stone replied. "Let's change the subject. I think we just had our first business discussion, if you don't count the part about your deceased husband. Josiah will be okay."

Tara appreciated the way he steered her back to the task at hand. "And you'll respect this—that I need to keep things strictly business?"

"Absolutely."

But the look in his eyes indicated he had more than just business on his mind.

"And what about after hours?" she asked, her emotions warring between accepting this attraction and fighting it with all her might.

He set his coffee cup down and came around the counter to where she perched on a bar stool. Touching a hand to her arm, he said, "That, too, will be up to you."

"Oh. Why?"

"Why what?"

"Why will that be up to me?"

Stone turned to lean back on the counter, crossing

his arms over his chest, an amused look on his face. "Well, I'm trying to gain both your respect and your trust, Tara. I won't do a very good job at either if I come on too strong, now will I?"

"But…" She sighed, attempting to regain control of her equilibrium. "I don't want you to even try, Stone. I was married to a man very much like you. That marriage almost failed because it was based more on lust then love."

He lifted a hand to his face, then brushed it down his chin. "Is that what you think? That I've just got the hots for you?"

She saw the disappointment in his eyes and wished she didn't have to be so honest. But if she'd been honest with Chad, things might be different now. "I just need to know that you'll do the right thing. That you'll respect my wishes regarding this whole arrangement."

Somehow, he'd managed to get even closer, the look in his eyes going against everything she'd just said. "And what are your wishes?"

Right now, she wished she could kiss him again. For a very long time. But, reminding herself that her next relationship with a man would have to be sincere and built on trust and love rather than just a physical attraction, Tara quickly pushed that fantasy away. "I wish that you'd understand I'm not ready for anything other than a business arrangement. A job."

His eyes searched her face. "That's all you need from me, right? A job. And a big check for your property."

"Yes," she said, trying to nod her head, trying to

find a good, strong breath to push at the denial. "I'm too tired and confused to deal with anything emotional right now."

"Do I make you emotional?"

He was doing it. Right here in her kitchen. He was pouncing on her without even touching her. Tara felt the heat from his eyes, saw the way his nostrils flared slightly as he leaned close.

"You…you make me crazy," she said.

"Define *crazy*."

"I don't know. The way you look at me. The way you kissed me the other night makes me think crazy things. Why are you doing that when we both know it can come to no good?"

"No good? Is that what you think being with me would be like, Tara? No good?"

Not really. She thought it would be not only good, but great. Wonderful. If she just leaned forward, she could be in his arms, safe and warm and overcome with a sense of belonging. But she couldn't do that. Not yet. Maybe not ever. "I just think we shouldn't rush into something we might regret," she tried to explain. "It's bad timing. I have to get my children back on a structured, calm routine. I have to pay off debts, think ahead to the future."

"I'm thinking of the future right now," he said, his hand snaking out to grab her arm. "The immediate future."

"Stone, don't. We can't."

He had her off the stool and in his embrace. "We can't what? Touch each other? Hold each other? Want each other?"

She tried to shake her head. "It's wrong."

"Why? Why is this wrong?" He pulled her close, but he didn't kiss her. "Is it wrong to want to *feel* something, Tara? Is it wrong to want something I can't even explain? Is it wrong to finally find a wonderful, interesting woman, a woman who outranks anyone I've ever known, and to want to get to know that woman, to help that woman, to protect that woman? Is that wrong?"

"Is that what you want?" she asked, her eyes touching on his. He looked so sincere, so secure in his longing, that she almost believed him. "Do you really want to get to know me, or do you just find me interesting and a challenge because I have something you want?"

"You mean the land?"

"Exactly."

He didn't answer her with words. He just pulled her close and kissed her. This kiss was slow and sweet and flowing, like a soft waterfall. She felt his hands in her hair, felt his touch on her lips, felt his need in the tender way he moved a finger down her face.

Then he lifted away and looked down at her. "I told you, I want more than just land now, Tara."

Tara whirled, then found her way to the other side of the counter. "And I'm telling you I can't give you anything more right now. I need a job. I need money. I need some peace of mind."

"But you don't need me, right?"

She did need him. But she couldn't let that happen right now. So she tried to explain. "I don't need the complications you bring, Stone." Lowering her head, she said, "I made a big mistake in marrying Chad too quickly. I just don't want to rush into another mistake. I won't do that again. And I won't put my children through that again."

"Okay." He backed up, swept a hand through his hair. "I'll expect a signed contract on my desk Monday morning. It'll take a few weeks to process the sale, but you can start to work right away. Give your boss two weeks' notice, Tara. Then report to work for me by the end of the month. You won't see me again until then, unless you decide you want to see me again. As I said, that's entirely up to you." He turned toward the back door. "Oh, and I had a nice time with you and the girls tonight. Tell Laurel I hope she'll eat a slice of that chocolate pie I put in the refrigerator."

Tara watched as he opened the French door, then closed it softly behind him.

Already the big spacious kitchen seemed empty with his leaving.

As did her heart.

"How could you do this to Daddy?"

The question, posed by Laurel at the breakfast table the next morning, threw Tara into a tailspin.

"What are you talking about?"

Laurel rolled her eyes, then threw down her half-eaten piece of toast. "I saw you last night, Mom. With *him.*"

Her heart accelerating, Tara motioned to Amanda and Marybeth. "Go get your backpacks. It's almost time for the bus."

"But—" Marybeth protested, staring intensely at Laurel.

"No buts," Tara replied. "I need to have a word with your sister, in private."

"Great," Amanda said, getting up from the table. "We never get to hear the good stuff."

"Just go, now," Tara ordered with a finger pointing toward the stairs.

The two girls stalked away, whispering to each other as they tossed curious glances over their shoulders.

"And don't try to listen on the stairs," Tara called.

Then she turned back to Laurel. "What do you think you saw, Laurel?"

Laurel sent her a chilling look through eyes made up too heavily with kohl liner and dark blue eye shadow. "I saw you kissing that man."

"Stone? You saw me kissing Stone?"

"Yes. He was all over you, Mom! And you won't even let me near Cal without a chaperon!"

Tara took time to count to ten and calm her nerves. "Were you spying on me, Laurel?"

"No!" She got up to slam her dishes into the sink. "I came downstairs to show you my outfit, to prove to you that it wasn't too skimpy. But when I got to the bottom of the stairs, I saw you with him."

"And what did you do then?"

"I watched, then I turned and ran back upstairs." She whirled to grab her suede purse. "You sure didn't waste any time."

Tara reached out a hand to her daughter. "Hold on. First of all, I am an adult and I have every right to date other people. Second of all, nothing is going on between Stone and me. I purposely told him last night that can never happen again.''

''You mean, you won't kiss him again?''

''Yes. That's what I mean.'' Tara motioned for Laurel to sit down. ''Honey, Stone and I are getting to know each other, and we're doing business together. He wants to buy my land—''

''Our land,'' Laurel said, her eyes flashing.

''Okay, *our* land,'' Tara corrected. ''And he's offered me a job.''

''A job?'' Laurel jumped up again. ''Mom, you can't work for him.''

''And why can't I? It would mean more money for us, a way out of our debts. I might be able to keep this house.''

''I don't care,'' Laurel said, her hands waving in the air. ''I don't want you around Stone Dempsey.''

Tara felt the weight of that demand down to her very bones. Laurel would never accept another man to replace her father. Which was why Tara could only concentrate on the job Stone had offered, and not the man who'd given her the job. ''I don't have a choice. I need to make enough money to take care of us, honey. Stone has offered me a good salary.''

''And what else is he offering, Mom?''

The sarcastic tone and the look her daughter sent with it only added to Tara's woes. ''Stone is trying to be a friend to us. That's all I can allow right now. But that doesn't mean you should be rude and disrespectful to either me or Mr. Dempsey.''

Laurel put a hand on her hip. ''Well, then, that also

means you don't have to go around kissing him, either. I hate him! I hate my life! And I hate—"

"Me?" Tara asked, tears brimming in her eyes. "Do you hate me, Laurel?"

Laurel grabbed her tote and books. "I have to go. The bus will be here soon."

"Laurel?" Tara called. "Laurel, we need to finish this conversation."

"I'm through talking to you," Laurel replied over her shoulder.

The next sound Tara heard was the slamming of the front door.

Shaking, Tara sank down on a kitchen stool, her head in her hands. "Lord, I can't do this anymore. I don't know where to turn. I don't know what's best for my family anymore. I need help."

She prayed that she was making the right decision regarding the new job at Stone Enterprises, working for Stone Dempsey. Working with Stone.

Tara realized she could be falling right back into the same pattern, the same trap that had brought her so much unhappiness in her marriage—being too ambitious and impulsive. Was she really taking this job for her family? Or was she taking this job just to be near him?

Chapter Nine

"Thank you for seeing me."

Tara waited for Rock to sit, then sank down on the wicker chair across from him. They were on the back porch of Rock's quaint cottage, which now served as a weekend home for Tara and the girls. Tara had left the girls in town with a neighbor so she could drive out here and have some quiet time with Rock.

Tara waved to the neighbor, Milly McPherson. Milly was out digging in her flower garden, a large straw hat plunked down over her gray bun. The old woman waved back, then went back to her task, her head down and her mind on the mums and pansies she was planting for some fall foliage.

"You sounded so upset on the phone," Rock said, his keen blue eyes moving over her face. "What's wrong?"

"Everything," Tara admitted. "I've tried to pray, but I can't seem to find the answers."

"Tell me," he said, his tone kind. "You know you can tell me anything."

"Yes, and I appreciate that," she said. "I hope my confiding in you hasn't put a strain on things with Ana."

He chuckled. "Ana knew she was marrying a preacher. I get phone calls night and day, from church members and people who want something fixed or built. Sometimes I fix cabinets, sometimes I try to fix confused souls." He shrugged, glanced out at the water. "I carry a lot of secrets close to my heart, Tara. But then, the Bible says 'for he knoweth the secrets of the heart'."

Tara looked out over the waters of the bay. It was a beautiful day, warm and humid, but with a gentle sea breeze. A colorful skiff sailed by like a quiet bird on the brilliant blue waters. "Does He know my secrets, Rock? Does God know that I'm trying to do what's best for my children?"

"I'm sure He does. What's this all about?"

"I'm going to take the job with Stone."

Rock's questioning expression changed to a frown. "Oh, I see. Have you told Ana?"

"No, not yet. But I told Stone yesterday. I won't start for a couple of weeks. I'll help Ana until the summer season is over."

"I'm not worried about you working weekends at the tea room," Rock said. "But I am worried about you working for Stone."

Tara knew Rock still had reservations regarding his brother. Well, so did she. "That's why I wanted to talk to you. Why wouldn't you want me to work for him?''

"Oh, I think that's fairly obvious," Rock said, his hands on the arms of his chair. "My brother and I have never seen eye to eye on things. Stone doesn't share my faith. He blames God for a lot of his misery."

"We've talked about that," Tara replied. "I think you're right, but I also think Stone is changing. He seems to be searching for something to fill his life."

Rock sat up, his eyes wide. "Are you telling me you've had a spiritual influence on my brother?"

"I'm not sure," Tara admitted. "But since we got past that first awkward, horrible meeting and all the contract negotiations, he's been nothing but kind to the girls and me—almost too kind. He could have demanded that I pay him the money Chad owed him. But he's willing to write that off as part of the package for the land."

"That and he gets you as part of the deal."

"That's why I needed to talk to you," Tara said. "Do you think, knowing Stone the way you do, that he's just using me to get at the land? Do you think he's being ruthless? Or is he being generous? He says it's not charity, but business. But could he really care about what happens to me and my family?"

Rock considered her questions a while before answering. "How important is this to you? I mean, how close have you and Stone become?"

"We're friends, business associates right now."

Rock leaned forward then. "I'm going to tell you this as a brother-in-law, not a minister. I don't trust

Stone. I've seen him in action before, and I've tried to give him the benefit of the doubt. But when Stone sets his mind on something or someone, he goes for it. And he doesn't stop to think of the consequences.''

"How can you be so sure?"

"Well, look at him. He's rich, and he didn't get that way by sheer luck. He has a reputation for leaving beautiful women along the path. He's been called hard-hearted by all the gossips, and he's been called the same thing by the entire Southern business community.''

"I never heard that," Tara said. "I've lived in Savannah for fifteen years and I never heard of him. Of course, I was lost in my own troubles during most of that time.''

"That's the other thing," Rock said. "Stone keeps a low profile. Doesn't it concern you that you didn't even know him before now?"

"A lot of businesspeople do that, Rock. They delegate jobs so they don't have to be everywhere at once. And I get the impression that Stone does that so he doesn't have to answer to the press or a lot of other people. Maybe so he doesn't have to answer to his family, either.''

"Well, shouldn't someone hold him accountable?"

Tara let out a sigh. "You know something? I asked you here to get advice regarding Stone. But I think you might be the wrong person to help me here.''

"Why would you say that?"

"Well, look at you. You're all in a fluster just discussing your brother. Rock, you are a kind, caring man, a minister to most of the people on this island.

Why can't you be the same with Stone? Everything you've just told me about your own brother is based on gossip and speculation. You should know the real Stone in your heart, shouldn't you? Or do you think you already do?"

He looked at her, realization dawning in his eyes. "You're right, of course. Goodness knows, I've tried to get past my resentment of Stone. I truly want him to be happy, Tara. But maybe I need to fix what's wrong inside myself before I condemn Stone any further."

"How can you do that?"

Rock shrugged. "Prayer. And I did offer to help him with Hidden Hill. I hear he's planning this elaborate dinner party to raise funds for the lighthouse, but honestly, I don't see how he'll pull it off. That house needs a lot of work."

"Oh, the fund-raiser. I'd forgotten all about that," Tara said. Just the thought of getting all dressed up to be with Stone caused her to go warm and soft inside.

"Are you going?"

"I hadn't given it much thought. But I guess if I take this job, he'll expect me to be there."

"Stone will expect a lot of things from you, Tara. Just remember that."

"You still don't trust him?"

"Do you?"

"I'm trying. He told me he wanted me to respect him and trust him. And he's not pushing for anything else right now." If she didn't count the way he kissed her.

Rock got up, put a hand on one of the porch railings. "Well, it seems you already believe in Stone enough to defend him against me. And maybe you're right. Ana says I have a blind spot regarding Stone. I'm beginning to think maybe she's got a point."

"You know she wants to get us together—Stone and me?"

"Oh, yes. She's mentioned it a few times. At first, I thought she just felt guilty. You know, since we're so happy—"

"I know. My sister and I have this history with Chad that won't let us give up completely on the past, but we've come a long way in being honest about that. Ana has a good heart—that's why she wants me to be happy. She wants me to find the kind of love she's found with you."

"I honestly don't know if Stone can give you that. I don't know if my brother is capable of real love and commitment."

Tara got up to stand beside him. "Well, I know I'm not going to rush into anything. You know about my life with Chad. I loved him, but it was more of a physical attraction. Our marriage wasn't built on solid ground and it almost destroyed us."

"You thought he was still in love with Ana."

"Yes, but…Chad loved me, too. I can see that now. I just didn't give him much of a chance to prove it. And, I was the same way you are with Stone. I didn't look deeply enough to even know my own husband. I regret that so much. I guess that's why I'm curious about Stone. He reminds me so much of Chad at times."

"So now you're afraid to fall for someone who is so much like your late husband?"

"Yes," she said, bobbing her head. "You do understand."

"Of course. And I think you're wise to take things slow." Placing a hand on her arm, he added, "I'll make you a promise. I'll try to extend the olive branch to Stone and look for the good that you see in him, if you'll be very careful and very honest in your relationship with him. Don't let him hurt you, Tara."

"I won't," she said. "But I worry about Stone getting hurt, too."

"That's a first," Rock said as he started down the steps. "And I have to admit, I've never thought of it in that way." Then he stopped to look back at her. "I've hurt my brother all these years, haven't I?"

"I think so," she said, hoping she was doing the right thing by telling him that. "I think Stone needs a brother—not a preacher, not someone to tell him what he's been doing wrong, but just a brother."

"I can try to be that," Rock said. "If it's not too late."

"God gives us second chances. That's what you told me, remember?"

"Oh, I see," Rock said, grinning. "You're using my own platitudes to get back at me."

"No, I'm giving you the same good advice you gave me. You've helped me so much, Rock. Why not do the same for your brother?"

"Ah, but *you* needed my help," Rock pointed out.

"So does Stone," Tara replied. "Even if he won't admit it."

"I'll see what I can do," Rock said, waving to her as he walked toward the chapel.

"See what you can do about that broken tree limb," Stone told the men he'd hired to clear the gardens at Hidden Hill. "This place has to be ready in two weeks."

"You gotta be kidding," one of the workers said to no one in particular.

"I'm serious," Stone explained in a calm, authoritative voice. "The house won't be finished, of course. That could take years. But I intend to have the gardens in some sort of shape for this gala." Then he smiled. "Relax, it's a garden party. And it will be at night, underneath the stars. We just have to pull out the bramble and brush and make sure we have things cleared for the tents and the stage."

"You're hauling a stage in here?" the supervisor asked.

"For the musicians," Stone explained, his patience stretching thin. "Just do it, guys. You'll get paid extra if you just follow orders and stop asking questions."

"Yes, sir."

"You have a way with words," a voice from behind him said.

Stone turned to find Rock standing by an ancient camellia bush. "Oh, great. You again." At least his brother didn't have the usual look of disgust on his face.

"Yep," Rock said as he strolled through the

patches of limbs and shrubs the men had already
cleared away. "Do you think you'll actually have this
place in shape for a big party in two weeks?"

"I'm planning on it," Stone replied, the list in his
head reminding him to check and see if Diane had
consulted with the caterers and florists on all the last
minute details. He braced himself for the onslaught
of his brother's disapproval, but was surprised by
Rock's next words.

"How can I help?"

Stone held a hand to his ear. "Excuse me? I don't
think I heard you right. Did you offer to help me?"

Rock looked down at the ground. "I've offered before, haven't I? I'd really like to help, Stone."

"Okay." Stone turned back to supervising the tree
cutters so his brother wouldn't see his surprise and
doubt. "Go ahead and take down that pine, too, Mike.
Looks like the pine beetles got to it."

Mike nodded, then started issuing orders.

Satisfied, Stone pivoted back to face Rock. "Want
to see the house?"

"Sure."

He took his brother up the winding stone staircase
to the second-floor terrace. The wide terrace formed
a cover over what had once been a carriage drive
leading to the back of the house where the kitchen
and servants' quarters had been built on the bottom
floor.

Stone waved a hand down toward the sounds of
power drills and hammering. "I'm redoing the
kitchen, then turning the rest of the lower level into
an office and game room."

"With a pool table?" Rock asked, hopeful.

"Of course. But I'll still beat you at eight ball."

"Probably. I'm a bit rusty since our days at the arcade on the boardwalk."

"Is that place still there?"

"No. Now there's some sort of galactic bowling and several fancy computerized game machines. The kids love it."

"I loved the arcade," Stone said, remembering how they'd hung out there during the summer when they weren't working.

"Why did you buy this place?" Rock asked as they entered through the open paneled doors.

"I wanted it," Stone replied. He didn't owe his brother any explanations.

"Remember washing all this glass?" Rock asked as he lifted his head up to the ceiling. "I think I counted all the panes in this room once—let's see, twenty panes per door and window times ten."

"Two hundred," Stone said, nodding. "I never counted them, but I've had to replace about half of them." Then he put his hands on his hips and stared at his brother. "I can promise you this. I will never have to wash them again."

"Then you bought the house out of revenge?"

He shrugged. "Maybe. Look, Rock, did you really come here to help, or to question my motives again?"

"A little of both," Rock admitted. "I had a long talk with Tara yesterday afternoon."

Stone hid his concern by holding up a hand. "Spare me the lecture, then."

"I didn't come to lecture. I said I came to offer my help. Didn't I already tell you that?"

"Let's get something to drink," Stone suggested, just to take the edge off seeing his brother here. Just to take the edge off knowing that Tara had talked to Rock about him.

Rock followed him through the drawing room—what was now going to be a huge den—and over to a massive Rococo sideboard that Stone had had restored to its former gilded glory. "Want mineral water or a soft drink?"

"Water," Rock said, his gaze moving over the high, mirrored walls. "This place always was excessive."

"And I aim to keep it that way. I'm living in these two rooms right now." He waved a hand over the big den. "I have a cot in the room that used to be the library."

"So you're The Great Gatsby now?"

Stone had to laugh at that. "Okay, maybe not quite that rich and forlorn, but I'm comfortable. Plus, I don't plan on winding up dead in the swimming pool."

"Let's hope not," Rock said as he took the crystal goblet of water from Stone. "About Tara—"

"We're going into a business arrangement, nothing more."

"Are you sure?"

"Is it any of your business?"

"She came to me for advice—"

"And you told her to steer clear of me?"

"No, as a matter of fact, she turned the tables on me and gave me some solid advice."

"To mind your own business?"

Rock shook his head, took a sip of his water. "She told me that I should give you the same consideration I do the rest of my congregation. That I shouldn't listen to the gossips. She said I should start being a brother to you again."

Stone gave Rock a long, direct look while he let that soak in. *Tara had defended him.* It was such a foreign concept that it took him a minute to realize the implications. She cared. About him. Maybe. "And did you set her straight? Did you tell her that you have always and will always disapprove of me?"

"No, but she pretty much pointed out the fact that I act that way. I guess I have been full of sanctimonious pride when it comes to you."

"That's a good word for it," Stone said, not even daring to hope that Rock might actually be trying to make amends. "Mind telling me why you feel that way about me?"

Rock glanced around. "Can we talk?"

Stone pushed a hand over his hair. "Brother, that's all I've ever wanted to do." He indicated a long brown leather couch centered in front of the huge fireplace. "Have a seat."

Rock sank down on the couch, while Stone took a matching overstuffed chair. "Stone," he began, his hands clasped together, "I haven't been a very good brother to you. All these years since you left to make your way, amass your fortune, whatever you want to call it, I've resented you."

"You resent my money?"

"No," Rock said and Stone saw the sincerity in his eyes. "I thought about it after I talked with Tara, prayed about it, and now I can see I resented that you left. That you went away, to begin with. I guess I wanted you to stay and fight right along with me."

"Fight what?"

"Our mother, our life. Our childhood," Rock said on a shrug. "I don't know."

"Clay left," Stone pointed out. "You still get along famously with him, don't you?"

"Yes, but Clay never rebelled the way you did. I always felt so responsible for you."

"Hey, I take responsibility for my own actions."

Rock looked up then. "I think that's what I resented the most. You were free, Stone. Free to go. Free to explore that big world out there. You didn't let our childhood woes hold you back."

"While you felt trapped?"

He nodded. "I'm not very proud of it, but after I talked to Tara, I realized that has to be it. I don't begrudge you making a living. I just begrudge that I never had the guts to try that myself."

Stone shook his head, his soda bottle dangling from one hand. "Rock, you've made a name for yourself here on the island. Man, you're a great carpenter and furniture maker, and what I hear, a passable preacher. And you are married to one of those pretty Hanson women. What more could you want?"

"I am happy now," Rock said, his eyes lighting up. "And I have Ana to thank for that. She makes me a better person, which I guess is why I'm here.

She's been encouraging me to talk to you. And now Tara's done the same.'' He paused long enough to inhale a deep breath. "Sometimes, God sends us answers to our prayers. But not always in a way we want to hear. I've been blind and stubborn, but now I can see clearly. I want to make things better between us, Stone. Will you let me try again? Will you give me a second chance to be your big brother?''

Stone sat there, leaning back in his chair, his eyes centered on his brother. After a long silence, he said, "Wow, those Hanson sisters are a force to be reckoned with. They actually have us in the same room, talking instead of fighting.''

"Does that mean you're willing to meet me halfway?'' Rock asked, extending a hand.

Tara had fought for him. The least Stone could do was make her proud, show her her efforts had not been in vain. Stone reached across and shook his brother's hand. "That means I'm glad you stopped by. But it also means the subject of my relationship with Tara is off-limits, agreed?''

Rock shifted, sighed, then nodded. "I think I can live with that. Just—''

"I won't hurt her, Rock.''

Rock finished off his water. "Okay, then. End of discussion. But if you need me—''

"I'll let you know,'' Stone said, still on shaky ground.

They sat in silence for a few minutes, the sounds of construction echoing up to them through the open doors. Off in the distance, Stone could hear the sea crashing against the shore. He felt like that beachhead out there. Since he'd met Tara, he felt as if he were being assaulted and rearranged, then shifted and washed clean again.

"Nice mantel," Rock finally said, nodding toward the bronzed marble over the fireplace.

Relaxing, Stone said, "Thanks. It has a certain quaintness about it."

Rock grinned then. "So you do have a sense of humor after all."

"There's a lot about me that you don't know," Stone pointed out.

"Ah, but there's a lot about you I do know, too," Rock said. "I remember how you used to catch blue crabs and steam them up for dinner on those nights when Mother was out in her studio."

"When was Mother *not* out in her studio?"

"Good point." Rock sat silent for a minute, then said, "And I remember how one year you wanted to grow the perfect orchid, for Mother's Day."

Stone lowered his head. "I was hoping she'd notice."

"But we couldn't get it to bloom."

"Nope. It just sat there, all green and spindly."

"And you never even showed it to her."

"Can I show you something now?" Stone asked, his heart pounding with the force of a breaker as that memory came crashing down on him. That Rock had remembered, too, only added to his confusion. Was God trying to send him a message?

Rock lifted his brows at his request. "You don't have a mad wife in the attic, do you?"

He laughed. "No. As the rumors go, I leave behind

a trail of broken hearts in my wake, but I haven't resorted to locking women in the attic.''

"Okay, so what do you want to show me?"

"C'mon," he said, lifting off his chair to take Rock's empty water glass. "Now, try to keep an open mind about this, okay?"

"Sure," Rock said as they entered a long wide hallway. "Are you taking me to the dungeon?"

"No, the solarium in the south wing."

"What's it like to live in a house that actually has wings?"

Lonely, Stone wanted to say. But he didn't. "Don't know. This is the first time I've actually stayed here since I bought the place."

"'A house is not a home'," Rock said, then winced. "Sorry."

"I figured you'd start quoting somebody or something sooner or later," Stone said, wondering why it had taken a word from Tara to bring his brother to visit. And wondering, too, if maybe she could bring some good to his life simply by being in it. "You're right, though. This is a long way from being a home."

"So I'll ask it again. Why did you buy this place?" Rock said as they entered the square, arched solarium.

"'I had a lover's quarrel with the world'," Stone responded.

"Robert Frost," Rock noted with a wry smile. "Not bad."

"You're not the only one who reads books, Rock." Enjoying the awakening expression on his brother's face, he pointed toward a long potter's bench nestled underneath a row of windows across the way. Lined up on the bench in varying stages of growth, sat several exotic orchids from around the world, some bright with flowers, some waiting to bud and open. "And you're not the only one who remembers that orchid that never bloomed."

Chapter Ten

"So this is it?" Tara asked a few days later.

"This is it," Stone replied.

They were back out at the land. They had decided to meet here to sign the initial contract. There would be other papers to sign later back at Stone's office, with Griffin Smith and Diane Mosely as witnesses. But right now, Stone wanted Tara all to himself.

This seemed like the best place to guarantee that.

"I see you didn't put in that clause I had requested," she said as she skimmed the papers in her hand through a chic pair of black retro reading glasses.

Stone enjoyed just looking at her. She was like a ball of golden fire, very elegant and sophisticated, but all action, always moving. Today, she wore crisp baggy olive green pants and a stark white cotton button-up shirt. Her blond hair fluttered in the humid breeze.

"Stone?"

"Hmmm?" He refocused then remembered her statement. "Oh, if you mean the clause about you never wanting to see me again, no, I definitely did not put that in the contract. I'd rather give up this land then have that happen."

Tara took off her glasses, her sky-blue gaze hitting him square in the face. And the gut. "You don't mean that."

He moved to where she leaned against her car. "Yes, I do."

She began to fidget, her hands moving through her hair. "You *can't* mean that."

"Why can't I?"

"Because we had another agreement, remember? To keep things professional. Stone, if you're going to make moves on me, then I won't come to work for you."

He did make a move toward her, his hands locking over each of her wrists as he urged her to him. "I want you to come and work *with* me, Tara. *With* me. There is a difference."

"Not really," she said, a little breath leaving her body. Then she looked up at him, her eyes open and questioning. "Why, Stone?"

"Why, what?"

"Why are you doing this?"

"You mean this," he said as he lowered his head to nuzzle her jawline. "Or this maybe?" He kissed her with a slow, steady, lingering touch. Then he lifted his head. "I would think that is obvious. I like kissing you."

"But you can't, we can't—"

Frustrated, and knowing she was probably right, Stone backed away. "Okay, okay. But I have to tell you, Tara, it's going to be extremely hard to work with you every day and not want to touch you or kiss you."

"Then maybe I'd better not sign this. You can have the land, Stone. But maybe you'd better not include me in this package deal."

"Is that what you think about me?" he asked, the old hurts surfacing. "You think I'm using you to get to the land or something?"

"Are you?"

His short laugh was brittle with anger. "Tara, think about it. It's more like I'm using the land to get to *you.*" Raking a hand through his hair, he said, "Up until I met you, I always let Griffin and other qualified people handle the details for me. It was all about the quest. I always went after projects, then sat back to watch what I wanted to happen become a reality. But not this time. This time, I've put myself on the line. I'm finishing what I started, Tara. With a hands-on approach."

"You can say that again," she told him, looking down at his hands as if remembering how they'd just touched her. Then she turned to stare out over the marsh. "I just don't know what you want, Stone."

Stone stood there, staring at her back. "Honestly, I don't know what I want, either," he finally said. "I used to know exactly what I needed. I set out to make a living for myself after college. I worked hard to form Stone Enterprises. My companies have a solid reputation in the construction and commercial real estate market. I have money, power.'' He stopped, a rush of breath leaving his body. ''I *had* control.'' Then he touched a hand to her arm, forcing her back around. ''But I don't have control with you, Tara.''

''So it's the thrill of the chase?'' she asked, the pain in her eyes making him flinch. ''Once I sign on the dotted line, you win and the game's over?''

''No,'' he said on a soft plea. ''That's my whole point. This isn't a game.'' He dropped his hand away. ''I just want to get to know you. Now you tell me, why that can't happen? Is it that you don't feel the same, that you don't want me around? Is it that I remind you too much of your husband? Or is it just that maybe you're a lot like me? That you have to be the one in control?''

''Maybe so,'' she said, her weariness apparent in the way she slumped back against the car. ''I thought I was in control all during my marriage, but I wasn't. And now I'm finding out even more things I never knew about my own husband. It wasn't enough that I believed he was in love with another woman.''

''Wow, back up,'' Stone said, throwing up a hand. ''You need to explain that for me. Did Chad…did he have an affair?''

She shook her head, dread evident in her eyes. She didn't want to tell him anything more about her marriage. She still didn't trust him, obviously. But she surprised him with her next words. ''Chad didn't cheat on me. But I had my doubts about him just the same. He dated Ana in college, before I came into the picture.''

"And?" Stone waited for her to finish the story.

"And I wasn't sure if he ever got over her." She sighed, shifted her feet. "Look, that's another story. It's just there was so much about Chad that he kept hidden. He kept it all inside." Glancing around, she said, "I never even knew there was a chapel on this place. And now I find out Chad used to visit it on a regular basis. He never even told me that, Stone. We never communicated. Neither of us was ever in control." She looked up then, a hand to her mouth as tears started misty in her eyes. "I'm so afraid I'll make another mistake. My children can't afford another mistake."

Stone put a hand to her hair and pulled her close. Although he was beginning to see why her trust was so hard to come by, he wouldn't question her anymore about Chad right now.

His eyes centered on hers, he said, "I promise you, this won't be a mistake. And if it means keeping your children safe and cared for, then I'll step away. I'll give you the job, with no strings attached. We'll develop this land together, no strings attached. But don't shut me out of your life. Just do the right thing. Sign the contract and I'll back off." He brushed a tear off her cheek, then added, "I know what it's like, Tara. I know what it's like to be a child and to be scared, with no money and no way out."

She didn't pull away as he'd expected. Instead, she started to cry. "Stone, I—"

He took her into his arms and held her and let her cry. "It's okay. It's okay. I can't explain my actions, but I will honor my promise. I won't push you any-more. Okay?''

She nodded against his cotton shirt and Stone felt the damp mist of her tears flooding right over his heart.

Then she pulled away, turned and signed the contract.

Tara felt drained. She'd cried so many tears and she didn't understand why, today of all days, she'd had to fall apart. And she didn't know why it felt so good to have Stone holding her, letting her cry. He hadn't made any demands, hadn't tried to kiss her again. He'd just held her. That meant more to Tara than anything else he could have done.

''I'm sorry,'' she told Stone as they started back toward their cars.

''For what?''

''For being such a big baby. I don't usually resort to tears when trying to make a decision.''

Stone opened her car door for her. ''I don't remember ever seeing my mother cry. Don't apologize for being human, Tara.''

Thinking that was an odd statement, Tara didn't question him. She let her gaze roam over the marsh and woods. ''Well, now, I guess this is one burden lifted off my shoulders. But you know something, I kind of hate to see this land changed. Chad loved it the way it is now, wild and free. He wanted us to build a house right here on this bluff.''

''We'll build lots of houses here,'' Stone said. ''Together.''

"So, do I report directly to you next week?"

He nodded. "Unless you'd feel more comfortable working with someone else."

Tara thought the last place she needed to be was near Stone Dempsey. He was confusing her with his words and his promises. He was such a paradox. At times, ruthless and direct, at other times vulnerable and evasive. Fascinating. And too dangerous. "I'll be all right," she said. "Just as long as you understand—"

"I do," he said, but the look he gave her was filled with regret. "I gave you my word."

"Okay, then. I'll see you soon."

"We have to finish up the paperwork back at the office. Say, Friday afternoon?"

"That's fine." She started to get in the car, then glanced down the trail leading to Josiah's house. "What about Josiah?"

"I don't know yet," Stone said. "I thought I might walk back there and talk with him."

Surprising herself, Tara said, "Maybe we should go see him together."

Stone looked at his watch. "I've got some time right now. Want to see if he's around?" He glanced down at her shoes. "It's not a long walk."

"In high-heeled pumps, you mean?"

He grinned. "Well, they're pretty but they sure don't look sensible."

Tara laughed, glad to be back on safe ground. "Women never buy sensible shoes. Don't you know that?"

"Know it and appreciate it," he said, his eyes still

on her feet. "But don't expect me to carry you all the way back here if you get blisters."

Knowing he'd have no qualms about doing just that, she said, "I won't."

She locked the car then followed him to the trail. They walked along in silence for a few minutes, the heat of the afternoon filtering through the shade of old, moss-covered oaks and knot-kneed cypress trees. Up ahead, a spray of tiny black insects whirled by like a cyclone. The marsh was filled with sounds and sights—insects buzzing, birds calling, fish jumping. Tara didn't want to think about snakes and alligators.

"Stone," she said after they rounded a curve, "thank you."

"For what?"

"For agreeing to my terms."

"Oh, that." He gave her a sideways look. "I'm regretting that already. But I'm learning to be patient."

"It's going to be a long haul," Tara said, wishing she could just let go and enjoy being with him. "But it's really important to me to learn restraint."

"Guess I need to learn that myself." Then he stopped in the road to look over at her. "And I owe you a thank-you, too."

"It's my turn to ask what for."

"For standing up for me to my brother."

"Oh, Rock told you that?"

"He didn't divulge any confessions, but yes, he told me that you defended me. No one's ever done that for me, Tara. Thank you."

Tara's heart soared with hope. ''Maybe we can work together and be good friends, after all.''

''If that's what you want.''

''I'm like you. I don't know what I want.''

''Then we'll go slow and figure things out together. And when you're ready—''

''I know where to find you.''

And she would find him, Tara thought. She'd be very careful in discovering the real Stone Dempsey. She'd learn all about the man behind the myth. Maybe then she could regain some of that control she lost each time he looked at her. Maybe then, she could follow her heart and grow closer to Stone.

Dear God, show me the way, she prayed. *I need to do the right thing this time. No more mistakes, no more regrets.* She'd married Chad on impulse, and while she regretted that, she couldn't regret the life that had brought her three beautiful children. But Tara refused to be impulsive again.

''There's Josiah's house,'' Stone said, bringing Tara out of her silent prayers.

She glanced up to find a weathered shack on stilts sitting haphazardly out over the marsh. ''He lives in that?''

Stone nodded. ''And seems to love it.''

''But it's barely standing.''

''It has a small bathroom of sorts and running water, but he doesn't have electricity. Says he doesn't need it.''

Tara shook her head. ''I didn't know people still lived this way.''

Stone guided her toward the rickety porch. "Over there is the chapel."

She turned to the right and saw the small white building. "How quaint. It looks like a child's playhouse."

"And not much bigger," Stone said. "But it's a pretty little thing. Very peaceful."

"You've been inside?"

"With Josiah."

Needing to know, Tara asked, "What did you feel when you went into the chapel?"

Stone smiled. "I felt a sense of peace. I felt as if everything would be all right."

"But you don't—"

"Attend church? Believe in God?" He shrugged. "God didn't do me many favors when I was growing up. I've had a grudge against Him ever since."

"And now?"

"And now, I think maybe it's time for God and me to come to terms." Stepping on the cracked concrete block that served as a porch step, he said, "I have everything a man could ask for, except someone to share it with. That gets a man to thinking, you know."

Tara nodded, feeling the sweet intensity of his words. "And you and Rock...have you made your peace with each other?"

"I think so," he said. "He's coming out to the mansion this weekend to help us get things cleared and cleaned for the benefit."

"About that—"

"You will be there. As a representative of Stone Enterprises, of course."

She accepted the order of boss to employee, even if she didn't trust his motives in using it. "Of course."

As if reading her mind, he said, "And you will be there on your own. I won't force you to be my date for the evening."

The sense of disappointment she felt was acute but necessary. She'd asked him to give her some time. He was only doing what she had requested.

Stone waited, as if expecting her to protest. When she didn't, she saw a flash of disappointment moving like a cloud cover over his silver eyes. He went up onto the porch and knocked on the door. "Josiah, are you in there? It's Stone Dempsey. We need to talk."

Then Tara heard it. A soft moan, coming from behind the house. "Stone, did you hear that?"

Stone was down the steps before Tara could turn around. Together they raced to the back of the tiny house.

"Stone, look," Tara shouted as she spotted Josiah lying in the duckweed at the water's edge. "It's Josiah."

"He's hurt," Stone said, running to the shoreline. He dropped on his knees in the mud beside Josiah, then pulled his cell phone out of his pants pocket. "Please, please let there be a tower somewhere out here," Tara heard him whispering.

Tara waited for Stone to speak into the phone. And while she waited, she prayed for Josiah Bennett to be all right.

"I can't get a signal," Stone said, throwing his phone down in disgust. "And he's hurt bad." He held up a hand to show Tara blood. "He must have hit his head."

"Josiah?" Tara said, leaning down beside Stone. "Can you hear me?"

Josiah tried to speak. "Fell down. Slippery."

Tara glanced around, seeing the marks of where the old man must have slipped in the treacherous mud. Then she saw the jagged piece of concrete beside Josiah's still body. "Stone, there's blood on this broken block. He must have hit his head on that."

Josiah managed a nod. "My fault. Left the thing there. Stepping stone."

"We'll have to get him to a doctor," Stone said, already reaching to scoop up the frail body.

"Wait," Tara cautioned. "Josiah, where do you hurt besides your head?"

Josiah swallowed, grimaced. "My insides."

"That's not good," Stone said, feeling for a pulse in Josiah's neck. "I don't know. His pulse seems weak."

"Okay, how do we get him out of here?" Tara asked, looking around.

"You stay with him," Stone said, getting up, his trousers muddy. "I'll go get my SUV and bring it back here."

"Okay," Tara said. "Just be careful. It's muddy in places along that lane."

Stone nodded, tossed her the phone. "Keep trying, just in case."

Tara took the phone, her hand still on Josiah's arm.

"It's okay, Josiah. We're going to get you to a hospital."

"You're Tara."

The statement made Tara stop punching buttons on the useless cell phone. Surprised, she said, "Yes, I am. Sorry to meet you like this, though."

Josiah managed a weak smile. "God sent me two angels."

Tara didn't know about that. It seemed highly unlikely that God would choose Stone and her to be angels. But she supposed stranger things had happened. If they hadn't been here today, who knew how long Josiah would have lain here, hurt and weak. And with all sorts of predators creeping around. She took a deep, calming breath and blocked out what might have happened if they hadn't found him. Then needing to talk, she asked, "How long have you been lying here?"

"'Bout two hours, I reckon."

She fanned a hungry mosquito away. "Have the bugs been bothering you?"

"Snake crawled across my foot," Josiah answered, causing Tara to jump. He actually chuckled. "He's long gone."

"Oh, good," Tara said, looking around in the weeds and grass. "At least you still have a sense of humor." To keep him still and awake, she asked, "Did a snake really crawl across you, or are you just joking with me?"

He grunted. "Snake came and went. Slid right over my foot. Big water moccasin, I think. I played dead and he kept on movin'."

"Let's not talk about that," Tara said, wishing Stone would hurry back. "How are you holding up?"

"Good, all things considered."

"How did this happen?"

Josiah swallowed again, pain etched in his face. "Old man, not watching where he was headed."

Went he started to cough, Tara hushed him. "Don't try to talk. Let me do the talking. You just nod, okay."

Josiah nodded, his chocolate-colored eyes on her face.

"The chapel is so pretty."

He nodded.

"It must be very old."

"Built by my ancestors."

"I told you not to talk," she gently chided.

His defiant grin was too weak to suit Tara.

"My husband Chad, he came to the chapel?"

Another nod. "He was lost."

Understanding what kind of lost Josiah meant, Tara felt tears pricking her eyes. "I wasn't a very good wife."

Josiah shook his head, his eyes widening. "Loved you."

Tara thought she hadn't heard him correctly. "Chad? Did you say Chad loved me?"

"Loved you. Didn't know how to show you."

"We should have talked more," Tara said, memories of their many quarrels echoing in her mind. "I should have been more considerate of his feelings."

Josiah grunted. "A hard case."

"You mean, Chad and me?" Tara lowered her

head. "We lost something, something that we could never get back. Now I'm afraid to ever go through that again."

Josiah stared up at her, his aged eyes seeming to see right through her fears and flaws. "Sow in tears, reap in joy. God gives second chances."

It was the same thing Rock had been telling her.

"I sure hope so," she said.

"You and Stone, reap in joy."

Tara wanted to set the old man straight, but then she heard the roar of an engine coming up the lane. "Josiah, Stone is back with his SUV. We're going to get you some help."

She felt Josiah's grip tighten on her arm. "God is helping all three of us today."

Tara didn't take the time to figure out what that statement meant. Stone parked the SUV, leaving the engine still running, and leaped out of the vehicle to open the door to the spacious back seat. Tara stood and watched as he lifted Josiah, careful not to hurt the old man, then gently lowered him onto the long seat.

"How you doing?" Stone asked Josiah.

Josiah grimaced again, then grunted. "Better now that I know."

"You're safe now," Stone said.

"Not just me," Josiah replied, a satisfied look replacing the pain in his eyes.

"What's he talking about?" Stone whispered to Tara as he rounded the truck.

"I have no idea," Tara replied.

But she was beginning to think she did have an idea.

Josiah was a very wise man. A man who listened to God and followed the word of the Lord. Somehow, she got the feeling that they had not only rescued Josiah, but that maybe they'd both been rescued by God and given that second chance everyone kept telling her about.

Chapter Eleven

The emergency waiting room at Saint Joseph's was clean and white-walled, with bright blue chairs centered at the information windows and bays of silk floral plants cascading from sleek countertops and tables along the walls.

Stone and Tara sat in two of the blue chairs now, waiting to find out about Josiah Bennett.

Tara nervously twirled the braided leather strap of her purse. "It's been a while, Stone. What could they be doing in there?"

Stone took her hand to stop her from fraying her expensive purse. "They're probably giving him a thorough examination." Then to take her mind off Josiah, he asked, "Did you get in touch with Laurel?"

Tara nodded. "They all made it home from school. I told her to sit tight until she hears from me again. And I called my neighbor and asked her to go and check on them."

"You don't like leaving your girls alone?" Stone asked, remembering how he and his brothers had often been left to their own devices while their mother worked.

"Not unless it's an emergency," she answered, waving her hands in the air to indicate this was just such a time.

Stone grabbed one of her hands, taking it in his again. "Calm down. He's going to be all right."

"I know," she said, weariness apparent in the dark smudges of fatigue underneath her luminous eyes. "I just don't like hospitals."

"Who does?" Stone asked. "I guess you're remembering Chad, right?"

Tara nodded. "They…they brought him here, too. I sat right over there by the door, waiting for the rest of the family to get here. He died before the girls got to see him."

Stone shut his eyes for a minute, the pain on her face too much to bear. Maybe because he was remembering that same familiar pain himself. "A child never understands death, no matter how hard people try to explain. I never got to tell my father goodbye, either." He didn't tell her that he often stood up on the terrace of Hidden Hill looking out to sea because that's where his father's remains rested, somewhere out there in that dark ocean. It was something that gnawed at Stone like unfinished business.

"I'm so sorry." Tara gave him an understanding look that only added to his woes, then pulled her hand away and shot up out of her chair. "I can't go through this again. I mean, I don't even know Josiah that well, but he knew Chad. And he's lived on that land for such a long time. It's as if—"

"As if we were meant to know him?"

"Yes, yes," she said, pacing on the tiled hallway. "It's just odd that Chad never mentioned him, or that I didn't know he lived on the land." She stopped, pushed at her bangs. "But Josiah sure seems to have me pegged. He seems to think…Oh, never mind. I'm just so worried and tired, I can't even focus."

Stone stood, then pulled her back against the wall. "I told you, I'll take care of him. If he doesn't want to move off the land, we'll let him stay."

Tara lifted her head, her expression questioning. "And how will we do that? Build half-a-million dollar mansions around his little shanty?"

Stone shook his head, the image of that contrast somehow making him feel strange and disoriented. "No. I've thought about it. We can leave him a spot there by the river. We'll put up a security fence, to protect Josiah and the chapel—"

"And keep him and his chapel members out of the fancy neighborhood? That should go over well with the homeowners association."

Sighing, Stone lowered his head. "Can we not discuss this right now? Josiah is hurt. We'll figure out the rest later."

Tara nodded, her hands fluttering to her side. "I'm sorry. I sound petty, but honestly, I'm more worried about an old man living out in the marsh by himself than I am about how the homeowners are going to feel."

"I know that," Stone replied, loving the compassion in her eyes, which surprised him. He'd never been one for too much compassion before, or for believing in fate. "And I feel the same way. We'll figure out something. Now, will you please come and sit back down."

Tara followed him back to the chairs. Stone knew her well enough to tell by the way she kept pushing at her hair and adjusting her clothes and purse that her mind was racing.

"What?" he asked, his fingers laced with hers. "Look, if it helps to talk about mundane things so you can take your mind off being here again, then talk away."

"I've got so much to do," Tara admitted, obviously glad for the distraction. "I have to tell Ana that I'll only be working at the tea room through August. School starts soon and I don't want to have to cart the girls back and forth between the island and Savannah. At least now, with the new job, I won't have to work weekends."

"Ever again," Stone said with such conviction, her head shot up. "Not as long as you do the job I'm paying you for," he quickly amended.

"Okay." She gave him a lame smile. "It's going to be a challenge, working for you. You'll keep me on my toes, that's for sure."

Glad to see her smiling, he nodded. "You can count on that. I'll keep you busy—which seems to be the way you like to stay."

"I get jittery when I have nothing to do."

"We'll have plenty to do. First thing, I'll show you

the preliminary plans for the subdivision and shopping complex.''

''A perfect upscale world.''

''You say that with a bit of distaste.''

''It's just that Chad and I lived in that world. And it came tumbling down pretty fast.''

''I won't let our new world tumble,'' Stone said. ''I only invest in solid acquisitions, Tara.''

She looked over at him with such a pensive gaze, Stone thought she might start crying again. ''Do you ever wonder if we're doing the right thing?''

He saw the worry centered in her eyes. ''You mean with the land or us?''

''The land. I know all about us and that can never happen.''

''Oh, the land.'' He wouldn't argue about the other right now, but it would happen. He'd see to that, too.

''That land needs an overhaul. It's got potential. Lots of potential.''

''Then why didn't I have more offers for it?''

''Maybe because others couldn't see that potential the way I do.''

''So you see potential where most folks don't think there is any?''

''I do.'' He let his gaze move over her face. ''Maybe that's why I'm so attracted to you.''

She frowned. ''Is that supposed to be a compliment?''

''In the best possible way. You've been down on yourself since Chad died, probably long before he died. Don't you think it's time you realized your full potential, too?''

Stone saw something change in Tara's vivid blue eyes, something subtle but sure. "Maybe you're right," she said finally. "I've always whizzed right through life, with very few downfalls or roadblocks. But all of that changed when Chad died. I had to face things I didn't want to face. And I lost my confidence. I felt like a failure, like I couldn't trust anyone to help me through the mess my life had become."

"And now?"

"And now," she said, her eyes full of sincerity, "I think I'm beginning to trust again."

"Me?" he asked, the one word full of hope.

"You," she answered softly. "And myself. And God."

Stone nodded, smiled. "Good. Then trust me in this one other thing, Tara. I will take care of Josiah. I won't let anything happen to him, okay?"

"Okay." With that she leaned back against the wall to wait for the doctors. And took Stone's hand back in hers while she waited.

That one small gesture of assurance and trust caused Stone to experience a flow of overwhelming emotions, emotions to which he couldn't yet put a name.

Except that…he thought it meant he might be falling in love.

"Wow, I can't believe that poor man lay there for hours," Ana said late the next afternoon.

Tara had come by the tea room to tell her sister that she could no longer help her on weekends. But first, she'd told Ana about finding Josiah out in the marsh. "I've never been so scared," she said now. "But thankfully, he's going to be okay. He has a concussion and two broken ribs, but no internal bleeding."

Ana turned around in her desk chair to stare at her sister. "And he has family coming to watch out for him?"

Tara nodded. "He has four children. Two sons who are both in the service—they can't get home right now. But the two daughters live pretty close—one in Atlanta and one in Tennessee. Thelma is coming from Atlanta tomorrow to take care of him for a while."

"That's good," Ana said. "Is he going back out to the marsh?"

"Thelma didn't seem to want him to do that. She told me on the phone that they've tried to get him to move since their mother passed away ten years ago. Can you believe Josiah and Dorothy raised four children in that tiny little house out on the marsh?"

"People do that all the time," Ana said, shrugging. "We just tend to not think about it or hear much about it."

Tara nodded. "But Josiah is different. I mean, to us, it looks as if he's living in poverty out there. But he seems perfectly content. He kept telling Stone and me that he had to get back to the chapel. He watches over that little church."

"Maybe that's why he doesn't want to leave," Ana said as she turned off her computer and called it a day. "Want a cup of cinnamon-apple tea?"

"That sounds so good," Tara said, following her across the hall to the kitchen, her mind still on Josiah.

"Stone said he will provide for Josiah, no matter what."

"He did?" Ana asked, her brows lifting. "Well, how about that."

Her defenses rising, Tara asked, "Does that surprise you?"

"It does, in a way," Ana admitted. "I guess based on what Rock had told me, I imagined Stone to be cold and self-centered."

"He's not," Tara said, too quickly.

Her sister stopped measuring out tea leaves to give her a long, hard stare. But instead of questioning Tara's declaration in favor of Stone, she asked, "So, do you think you'll enjoy working for Stone?"

"I think so," Tara replied, "now that we have an understanding."

"Oh, what kind of understanding?" Ana asked as she set out a tin of fresh tea cakes.

"We've agreed to keep our relationship strictly business."

"Really?"

"Yes, and don't give me that look."

"What look?"

"The look that says you don't believe me."

"Well, I don't believe you because I think there is much more to you and Stone besides work. But I promised Rock I would stay out of it."

"Thank you," Tara said, her smile soft. "And speaking of Rock, did he tell you that he and Stone resolved some of their differences?"

"Yes, he did, and I'm very happy about that. And Eloise is beside herself with joy, knowing that those two are finally coming around. Rock even went up to Hidden Hill yesterday to help the workers. He said the gardens look a lot better now that Stone brought in landscapers and hired a tree and lawn service to clean the place up.''

Tara took a sip of her tea, then broke off a piece of buttery cookie. ''Stone wants this gala to be a big event.''

''So you're going?''

''As an employee of Stone Enterprises, yes.''

''Oh, I see.''

''You're giving me that look again.''

Ana grinned. ''Am I?''

Tara chewed the rest of her cookie, then got up. ''Look, Stone and I are attracted to each other—''

''Gee, you think?''

''Yes, okay, but I'm not ready for all of that yet.''

Ana turned serious then. ''You mean because of Chad?''

Tara nodded, then looked down at the tile on the counter. ''There's so much inside me, Ana. Guilt, frustration, fear, pain. I don't want to make a mistake.''

Ana patted her hand. ''That's probably wise. You don't have to rush anything.''

''I'm not,'' Tara explained. ''And Stone has agreed to honor my request for time and space.''

Ana looked skeptical, but said, ''Maybe he is changing for the better. Rock seems to think he is, and Rock credits you with making that happen.''

''Me?'' Tara felt the shock of that down to her toes, right along with a warm feeling that left her both confused and elated. "I haven't done anything but try to be a friend to Stone, now that I've gotten to know him better."

Ana smiled, then bit into a cookie. "Well, maybe that's exactly what he needed, someone to believe in him, someone who sees his potential."

Tara remembered Stone's words to her at the hospital. "Stone told me I need to realize my full potential," she said. "Ana, do you think it's possible that God puts two people together to make them both better as a whole?"

Rock came into the kitchen before Ana could answer. Walking to his wife, he kissed her on the cheek. "So here you two are. What are you talking about—world peace or how to take over mankind?"

"A little of both," Ana said, grinning. "Tara just asked me a question I think only a preacher can answer."

Rock laughed, grabbed a cookie. "I'm not really a preacher, I just play one on Sundays. But I will try to answer your question."

Tara smiled. "You are more of a real minister, Rock, than some preachers who've been trained and earned their doctorate in religion, I think."

"Well, I'm honored you think that," Rock said, his eyes crinkling as he smiled. "What's the question?"

Tara repeated her question. "Do you think God has a hand in placing two lost souls together to find their way back—to make them better people?"

"Better as a whole," Ana added, repeating Tara's original question.

Rock glanced from his wife to his sister-in-law. "Is this a trick question?"

"No, I really need to know," Tara said, smiling at Rock's look of fear and dread. "Is it that hard to answer?"

Rock shook his head. "No, it's just that you two are a formidable duo. I don't want to say the wrong thing."

Ana patted his arm. "Relax, you're perfectly safe with us. I was just telling Tara that you think Stone has changed for the better, because of her. I think she's not quite ready to accept that she has made a difference in his life."

"It's just that it wasn't all me," Tara said. "Josiah made a strong impact on Stone, too."

"But you were there when Stone met Josiah, right?" Ana asked.

"Yes, but Stone and Josiah have a very unique relationship. It didn't include me until I agreed to work for Stone and then Josiah got hurt."

Ana waved a hand. "Okay, I can accept that. But let's get back to the question at hand." Turning to her husband, she asked, "Don't you think Tara has changed Stone?"

"Oh," Rock said, relief clear on his face. "The answer to your question is yes, absolutely." He paused a moment, then added, "My brother has been so distant and hard to deal with for so very long, both my mother and I are amazed that he's even speaking to us again."

"But wouldn't he have maybe started coming around, anyway?" Tara asked, wanting to make sense of things. "I mean, he was planning the gala for the lighthouse before I came into the picture. He would have had to run into both of you on the island anyway."

"True," Rock answered, "but before he was planning the gala for all the wrong reasons—he wanted to impress everyone on the island and he wanted to get next to my mother and me."

"And now?"

"And now," Rock said, taking another cookie in his hand, "Stone has truly changed. We've talked on several occasions since Ana first forced me to go out and see him at Hidden Hill, and especially since you and I had our own conversation about Stone. He's different now. He has more compassion for his fellow man. And he has a warmth in his voice whenever he mentions you, Tara. So yes, I'd say you've made a good impression on my brother. And I'd say God did have a hand in that, and in his meeting with Josiah, too."

Tara sank down on her chair. "But why would God choose me? For so long, I didn't put God at the center of my life. Why would He use me to change Stone for the better?"

Rock looked at Ana, then pulled his wife close. "Tara, think about it. When your life started spiraling out of control, what did you do?"

Tara sat there, seeing the happiness and contentment on their faces. Then it hit her. "I turned back to God. I turned the control over to Him." Tears springing to her eyes, she asked, "Rock, do you think because of that, he allowed me to help Stone, too?"

Rock nodded. "You opened your heart to God and now God is rewarding you by using you to help Stone. Tara, you've managed to do something I've been trying to do for years. You've made Stone more humble, more compassionate, more caring. And my mother and I are very thankful for that. I tried so hard, but something was blocking my heart. I still held resentment toward Stone. You could have felt that way, too, when he went after your land. But instead, you turned that around and tried to reach a compromise that worked for both of you. And the result is that you've become closer."

Tara felt such a lump in her throat, she couldn't speak. Finally she said, "But what if this backfires? What if Stone and I... What if he resents me for changing him?"

"Why would he resent you for making him a better person?" Ana asked.

Rock nodded his agreement. "Tara, Christ went out among the worst of society and brought blessings to those who thought they had nothing left in this world to give. They thought no one cared about them. But Christ did. Because you believed in my brother when others, including me, doubted him, he's seen something inside himself that he's kept hidden all these years."

"Don't give me so much credit," Tara said, getting up to pace the room. "Stone always had good inside him. He was just hiding it."

"Exactly," Rock said. "The scripture says no one should hide his light under a basket or in a secret place. By offering to defend Stone, by seeing the good he was trying so hard to hide, you've opened him up to the light.''

"The light inside him?" Tara asked, smiling at last.

"Yes," Rock said. Then he lowered his head. ''Sorry, I didn't mean to give a sermon right here in the kitchen, but it's true.''

Tara turned to face them again. "It is true. Stone has promised me he won't push me toward a relationship we might both regret. And he's promised me he'll take care of Josiah. I know there is good in him. I've seen it.''

Rock came around the counter and hugged Tara close. "Actually, I've seen it, too. Stone showed me something out at Hidden Hill the other day—well, I won't say what, but it really made me see I was wrong about so many things. My hard-hearted brother does have a few soft spots.'' He shrugged, lowered his head. "Miracles happen when we turn control over to God, Tara. And yes, I believe God brought you and my brother together for a reason. Now whether that leads to the two of you grower closer or just staying friends, I can't say. That will be up to you.''

"With God's help," Tara replied.

"With God's help," Rock answered.

Later that night, Stone stood on the terrace at Hidden Hill, looking out at the sea. He could hear the waves crashing against the dark shore, could see the whitecaps glistening in the moonlight just as they broke and lifted in a foamy song of never-ending anger and turmoil.

Stone felt some of that same anger and turmoil inside his heart. It was the same anger, the same turbulence he'd carried inside his soul since the day his father had disappeared out in those dark, unforgiving waters.

But tonight, right this minute, his heart felt a different kind of emotion, an emotion that softened the anger like the sea calming down after a violent storm.

Because of her.

Stone thought about Tara and wondered what it was about her that made him do things he'd never dreamed of doing before. She made him feel things he'd never felt before.

"Why is that, Lord?"

Surprised that he'd made that plea out loud, Stone glanced around. But he knew he was alone here in this big, old house. And he knew with a revealing intensity that much in the same way he was working to restore this house, someone, something inside him, was working toward restoring his own lost faith and crumbling, weak, foundation.

Then Stone heard it as if it had been spoken on the wind. Words his father had told him one day when he'd been allowed to go out on the shrimp boat.

"Why do you fish?" Stone had asked his dad.

And his father had answered, "'Come after me and I will make you fishers of men'."

Stone heard that verse now, clear and concise, as he stared out to sea. And he thought about the conversation he'd had with his father there on the boat, just a few weeks before his father had died.

"Do you know what that means, son?"

Stone had answered no.

His father had explained, "It means that Christ wants us to follow Him always, and to feed the souls of men, not just with fish or bread, but with the word of God. That's why I fish. I believe in God's bounty and I believe in sharing that bounty. It provides me with a good living and it provides nourishment for my table and for my soul. When I go shrimping, I provide a practical food for people to eat, but I also bear witness to the grace and goodness of God's vast ocean. Always be a fisher of men, Stone. Remember that."

Stone stood there in the darkness, a piercing pain of longing hitting him right in the heart. "I had forgotten, Daddy," he said to the wind. "I had forgotten."

And he'd blamed everyone, including God, for taking his father from him, for keeping his mother from him, for forcing Stone and his brothers to live in poverty, for making his childhood so hard and miserable.

But that was changing. Stone had reconciled things with Rock and his mother. He'd made promises to Tara, the kind of promises he'd never made to another woman. And here, tonight, he also wanted to make a promise to God.

For the first time since he was a child, Stone tried to pray. "Help me, God. Help me to find a way to make her love me." Stone lowered his eyes away from the sea. "Help me to find my way back to being a fisher of men."

Then he lifted his eyes up to the night sky. "With Your help, I know I can do this."

And with Tara's love, he could at last put the past behind him and be a better man. The type of man of whom his father would be proud.

Chapter Twelve

"And that's how they lived from the time they were freed until after the war was over. My people have always lived on the marshland. Always."

"Wow." Amanda sank back down on the stack of pillows around Josiah's feet. "I'm going to do my Georgia history report on this, Mr. Josiah. Think I'll get an A?"

Josiah laughed, then grimaced from the pain in his cracked ribs. "I reckon if you set the record straight, you'll gain more than a good grade, little lady. Not many people outside the Bennett descendants know about the story of the free men of color who lived on that land. That's why I have to go back and take care of the chapel—it's the only building left."

Tara saw the worry in Josiah's aged features, then glanced around Rock's cottage to make sure everything was in order. Rock had graciously loaned it to Josiah while he recuperated. His daughter Thelma and her two girls were spending the next week with Josiah here on the island. The girls, twins named Monika and Moselle, were close to Amanda's age, and had instantly hit it off with Tara's two youngest daughters. They now sat with Marybeth and Amanda at their grandfather's feet, listening to the colorful history of the Bennett clan. Laurel was with Cal at Eloise's house, but on a strict curfew to be home by seven.

"Daddy, I told you to quit worrying about the chapel," Thelma said. "We're going to drive out this afternoon and check on things for you."

"And feed that old stray swamp cat that roams around my house," Josiah reminded her again. "Scratch, he gets mighty hungry."

"I'm sure he has plenty to live off of in the marsh, Daddy," Thelma said, grinning and shaking her head at her father's concerned expression. "That cat is as old as me, and still kicking."

"Him and me," Josiah said, and then demonstrated by kicking both his skinny legs against the leather recliner he was lounging in. "Ouch," he said as the actions obviously caused his ribs to burn in protest.

"Daddy!" Thelma rolled her chocolate colored eyes, then tossed her brown curls. "See what I mean, Tara. The man is as stubborn as an old mule."

"But still kicking," Josiah said again. Only this time he didn't move one muscle except to smile.

Tara shook her head. "You are recovering remarkably. I can't believe just a few days ago, you were lying in that marsh—you scared Stone and me." She stopped, telling herself not to spoil the happy mood. "Well, I'm just glad you're getting better."

Josiah grunted. "I appreciate this nice, cozy cottage, Tara, but I sure miss my house."

Thelma shot Tara a knowing look. They'd been huddled together in the kitchen, trying to decide what was best for Josiah. Thelma didn't want him going back to the marsh alone, but Josiah didn't seem to want to live any place else.

Amanda and Marybeth turned back to Josiah. "Tell us some more about your great-grandfather Sudi, Mr. Josiah. About how he made a living from the marsh and the river after he came back from the Civil War."

Monika grinned up at Josiah. "Yeah, tell 'em how he fought in the war then came home and wrestled an alligator so he could feed his starving family."

Moselle gave her sister a long stare. "He didn't wrestle an alligator, Moni. It was a crocodile. There's a difference."

Josiah chuckled, holding his bandaged ribs. "Now you girls probably need to quit worrying about crocks and gators and help your mama and Tara get this place cleaned up. We don't want Mr. Rock to kick us out for being slovenly."

"Daddy, you haven't been slovenly a day in your life," Thelma said, fluffing pillows and straightening magazines as she went. "And you sure taught me to be neat."

"Hope so," Josiah replied, pride shining in his eyes. "Your mama, now that woman could keep a house so clean, you could eat peas and corn bread straight off the floor."

"Did you ever try that, Mom?" Moselle asked, laughing.

"No, honey. I'll just have to take your grand-daddy's word for it." Tara saw the pensive expression on Thelma's face. "But your grandmother Dorothy could surely cook. I wish she was still here."

"Me, too," Moselle said, then turned back to Josiah. "Do you miss her, Granddaddy?"

"Miss her every day," Josiah said, his eyes misty. "But I'm not worried one bit. I'll join my Dorothy in heaven soon enough."

Marybeth glanced up at Tara and the look in her eyes broke Tara's heart. "Will we see Daddy in heaven, Mom?" she asked.

Tara thought about that, about how she should an-swer her daughter's question. Panicked, she looked at Josiah. He nodded briefly. "Yes, honey, I'm sure we will. Josiah has told me things about your father I didn't even know. And they've brought me comfort. Your father visited Josiah a lot."

"He especially liked the chapel," Josiah said on a low voice. "Chad knew that God was watching over him."

"But we never went to church much," Amanda said, her gaze flying to her mother. "I'm glad we do now, though."

Josiah nodded, cleared his throat. "Going to church is good and I'm glad you're doing that now, but being in church and going to God are two different things, precious. Chad might not have graced the doors of the church, but he knew that God was there in that little chapel. He knew, because he sat and listened. That's all the Lord wants. He tells us to be still and know that he is God."

Amanda rubbed her nose. "So if I lay still at night and listen, God will be there? And maybe my daddy, too?"

Josiah nodded. "Yes, ma'am. No doubt in my mind." His aged eyes shifted to Tara's face, the question lingering there as if to say, "Do you still doubt?"

Tara glanced around the room, feeling as if the walls were closing in on her. "I—I'd better go check on the wash," she said. She hurried out onto the back porch and into the little room where the washer and dryer were stored. Then she heard a car pulling up, and glanced out the window to see Stone coming up the back steps with packages in both arms.

"Hi," Tara said as she came out of the laundry room and onto the back porch. "What are you doing here?"

"Good to see you, too," Stone said, his eyes moving over her face. "Are you all right?"

"Fine." Tara swallowed back the need to lash out at him. It wasn't his fault that her guilt about Chad colored every aspect of her life these days. But it was his fault that she couldn't stop thinking about Stone and the way he made her feel. "I've just been busy and worried and…so much is happening, so fast."

Stone set the grocery bags down on a cedar picnic table pushed up against the wall. "Hey, take a breath. Josiah is doing well and we're going to figure it all out."

Tara waved a hand in the air. "Figure what out? Where my life is going, what other secrets my husband kept from me, whether or not my oldest daughter will ever forgive me?" She stopped, took a long breath. "How I really feel about you? How am I supposed to figure all of that out?"

Stone grabbed her arm. "That's it. You need a break. I know you've been burning the midnight oil, trying to finish up with your commitments at work before you switch over to Stone Enterprises. And while I admire your drive, I also know that you can't handle everything at once, Tara. You need to rest."

"I can't," she said, her shoulders slumping. "I have to get back to Savannah tonight, to finish up some contract work for Monday. Laurel has a term paper due on Tuesday. Marybeth has a dentist appointment on Wednesday and Amanda has twirling practice on two of those days." Hearing laughter coming from the front of the house, she glanced inside. "At least Josiah is safe."

"Yes, he is," Stone said. "And that's one reason I came by. Thelma wants us to try to convince him to either move to Atlanta with her or stay here on the island where he'll have a clinic close by and neighbors to check on him."

"He won't do that," Tara said. "He wants to go home."

"Well, we'll just have to deal with it," Stone said. "I'll go in and visit with him, feel him out about things." He leaned close, assaulting Tara's senses with a clean, spicy smell that only reminded her of his masculinity. "And then, I'm taking you and the girls out to Hidden Hill for a picnic."

"I told you, I can't," Tara said, wishing she could take the afternoon off. But picnics were not part of her job requirement.

"What would it hurt?" Stone asked, his quicksilver eyes drenching her with a challenge. "You could spend time with the girls and we could just talk…about things, about work. Laurel can bring Cal. And if it will help, I'll even invite my mother. She's been hinting for a tour of the house anyway."

Tara shook her head. "I told you, I have obligations."

"The contracts can't be processed until Monday, right?" Stone countered.

"Right," Tara finally said, thinking if she went with Stone at least they could go over a few of the details of her job responsibilities. She thought about it for a minute, then said, "Okay, but only if we stick to discussing work." At his nod, she added, "I'll have to find Laurel first. And make sure Josiah is okay here."

"We'll bring him and Thelma and the girls with us," Stone replied, a light of adventure shining in his eyes.

"How are we supposed to concentrate on work with half the island going on this picnic with us?"

"We'll manage," he said, his gaze moving over her face in a way that made her feel edgy and flushed. "And besides, with all these folks there, maybe you'll relax and learn to trust me."

Tara laughed. "With that many chaperons, I'll be safe with you, maybe."

"Maybe," he said, his tone implying she'd never really be safe with him.

Stone turned to find Rock staring at him.

"What?" he asked before glancing back down to

the crowd of people centered on the back lawn of Hidden Hill.

"Who are you and what have you done with my brother Stone?" Rock asked, amazement evident in his blue eyes.

Stone managed a curt laugh. "Surprised?"

Rock nodded, took a drink of iced tea. "More like flabbergasted. I mean, look down there. Mother is here and smiling at Don Ashworth. My wife is dishing out cookies and lemonade with a grin. Cal and Laurel are beaming—Laurel's really pretty when she decides to smile. And Josiah and his family are laughing and telling tales to Tara's girls. Oh, and did I mention that Tara looks relaxed and happy, too? What have you done, Stone?"

Stone turned to lean against the cool bricks of the terrace banisters. He couldn't yet bring himself to discuss his epiphany with his brother. "You don't approve of this little gathering?"

"Oh, I approve," Rock replied. "It's just so—"

"Out of character for a self-centered man like me?" Stone finished, some of that old resentment and hardness bringing the wall back up.

"Well, yes," Rock said, nodding. "Don't get me wrong. I'm very happy to be here and even happier to be helping you get this place in shape for the lighthouse gala next week."

"But…?" Stone asked, thinking that in spite of all his good intentions, everyone around him still seemed to doubt him.

"But I have to wonder why you're doing all of this?"

Stone turned back to watch the crowd below. Instead of having a leisurely picnic with the food he'd had delivered from a local deli, they'd all pitched in and helped the ever present landscaping team with the gardens. He watched now as Tara and Ana sat in the dirt and grass, helping one of the landscapers plant colorful mums and pansies around an ancient cluster of camellia bushes. Off to the side, Cal and Laurel were helping Cal's father, Don, with a wheelbarrel full of compost. Even his mother Eloise was getting in on the act. She was clearing a spot in the center of the garden, directly in line with the restored pool, for the sculpture she'd given to Stone years ago. In storage now, the sculpture would gain a place of prominence in the gardens at Hidden Hill.

"I don't know," he admitted to Stone. "I'm a bit baffled myself." His gaze went back to Tara. He really liked watching her. She was like the wind, always in motion.

He could feel Rock staring at him. "You're falling for Tara, aren't you?"

Stone didn't answer. He looked down at the ice melting in his tea glass. "Maybe," he finally said, refusing to look Rock in the eye.

"Ana was right all along," Rock said, almost to himself, amazement in the words.

"What do you mean?"

Rock shrugged, popped a piece of ice into his mouth. "Ana thought you and Tara would be perfect for each other."

"Does she still think that?"

Rock gave him a grin. "Well, she's wavered some, having heard about your...uh...negotiations regarding Tara's land. But even though she's decided to back off, I think deep down she's still hoping you two will work things out in a romantic kind of way."

Stone let that settle around him, then asked, "What's the deal with those two and Chad, anyway?"

Rock squinted toward the western sun. "Tara hasn't told you?"

"Told me what?" Stone asked. "She's mentioned that Ana and Chad dated before he married her. But that's about it."

Rock nodded, then glanced down to where his wife and Tara stopped planting ground cover long enough to nibble on turkey club sandwiches. "I don't think I should talk about that. Tara will have to explain things."

Stone appreciated his brother's tact, even if it goaded him that he wasn't on the inside loop regarding Tara's past. "Okay. I guess she'll tell me if she thinks I need to know."

"Yes, she will," Rock replied, relief evident on his face.

Stone watched Tara now as she laughed at something Ana said. She had a thousand-watt smile. He was glad to see her happy. But was she really happy?

He'd abided by their agreement, biding his time until she felt she could trust him. He hadn't been overbearing about her finishing up work for her former boss, not in the way Stone was usually over-

bearing to new employees. He'd tried not to manipulate her into anything that would make her feel
uncomfortable, including coming here today. They'd
managed to have a thorough discussion about business, in the midst of all the people roaming around
the grounds, then he'd told her to "go play in the
dirt" with her sister and her children. Told her to go,
then wished desperately she'd invited him to come
and play with them.

He was going to try really hard to stay away from
her, except for necessary business decisions and dis-
cussions. He'd even had Diane place Tara's spacious
office down the hall on the far end of the building,
away from his own.

Unfortunately, his assistant wasn't buying that.

Still remembering Diane's words when he'd told
her he was hiring Tara Parnell, Stone had to smile.

"She won't give in to your charms, so you hired
her to work for you?" Diane had asked, grinning.

"Something like that."

"Griffin thinks you're going through some sort of
emotional crisis."

"Could be."

"Griffin says you've never been this involved in a
deal."

"Griffin gets paid to worry about business, not my
personal life. And so do you."

"Right," Diane had answered, not in the least
scared about telling him what she thought. "We don't
get paid to worry about you either, and we both do.
So, Stone, I'd like to say that I'm officially happy for

you, *and* worried for you. I think you've finally met your match."

Remembering that her eyes had held a tad too much open glee, Stone shook his head now. And again felt his brother watching him.

"You haven't taken your eyes off her," Eloise said from the steps, causing him to lift his head in her direction. Apparently, his mother had been watching him, too.

Rock chimed in. "I think my brother is slightly lovesick."

Eloise came to stand between them. "Just as you were earlier this year, if I recall."

"You are correct," Rock replied, his smile indicating that he still had it bad. "You should be proud, Mother. Two down, one to go. Clay had better run for cover."

"I am proud," Eloise said, her turquoise dream-catcher earrings jangling against her shoulders. "I'm proud that my sons have found two wonderful mates. And I'm very happy that we've all connected again, at last."

Stone felt the yoke of their expectations weighing heavily on his shoulders. "Aren't you two getting ahead of yourselves? Tara and I are friends. We're going to be working together, nothing more."

"Oh, really?" Eloise asked, her winged brows going up in surprise. "And do you stare at all of your employees in that same way?"

"I'm not staring," Stone said, trying to sound detached. "I'm enjoying my guests. *All* of my guests."

Rock gave his mother a warning look. "You are

staring, but you're also doing something that makes me think the old Stone is still warring with the new, improved model.''

"Oh, yeah, and what's that?"

Rock lifted a hand in the air. "You're still up here, looking down, brother. Don't you think maybe you should go down and join the crowd?"

Stone looked from his brother's questioning expression to his mother's prim, tight-lipped smile. "I hate it when you're right," he said.

Then he turned and hurried down the steps to Tara.

Chapter Thirteen

A storm was coming in.

Tara stared out at the blackening sky. "Maybe we'd better head back to Savannah."

Stone walked around the granite-topped counter of the long multiwindowed kitchen. Everyone else had left. The girls were watching a movie on the big screen television in the den. Well, Amanda and Marybeth were watching a movie. Laurel was pouting.

"Why the rush?" he asked, seeing the contrast of Tara's feminine warmth in this starkly decorated room.

Tara pivoted from her spot by a floor-to-ceiling bay window in what would soon be the redecorated breakfast room. "Rush? Stone, we've been here all afternoon."

"Tired of me already?"

"No, just plain tired," she said on a shrug and a yawn. "Sorry. I haven't dug in a flower bed in so long, I have muscles screaming in places I didn't even know I had muscles.''

Stone rounded the counter to push her down on a tall, steel-encased bar stool. ''Let me give you a neck massage.''

He saw the protest forming in her expression, but she sank down on the chair anyway. ''That sounds too good to pass up.''

Outside, a spark of lightning hit the dusk, followed by the rumble of thunder. Tara tried to bolt, but his hands on her neck held her down with a gentle persuasion. ''Sit. Relax. The storm will pass.''

''I don't want to drive home in the rain.''

''You don't have to.''

''Oh, and are you going to call me a taxi?''

''No. You can stay here as long as you like.''

He pressed his fingers against the soft skin of her neck, just above the pink cotton of her round-necked cashmere summer sweater. ''How's that?''

''That feels wonderful,'' she said, her head slumping forward just enough to allow him a peek of her slender neck. ''You could start your own therapy business, you know?''

''I only give massages to special people.''

He felt her tense. ''Am I special?''

''Of course you are,'' he said, his eyes enjoying the golden hues of her hair as it fell forward. ''Did you have fun today?''

''Mm-hm,'' she said, ''and so did the girls. Laurel even seemed to enjoy herself.''

''Until Don took Cal home.''

''Those two are becoming too serious, I'm afraid.''

Stone smiled to himself. "That's probably what this whole island is saying about us. Do you know we're the topic of the week?"

"Oh, yes. Eloise said that Greta Epperson person keeps buzzing around, wanting the scoop on us."

"Is there a scoop?" he asked, his heart tripping over itself as he took in the sweet floral scent of her shampoo.

She tensed again, then lifted her head. "Thanks," she said as she got up to roam around the work-in-progress kitchen. "All this steel and gray—you need some flowers in here, Stone."

"I need you in here," he said, his hands holding on to the counter as he stared across the room at her.

"We aren't supposed to be having this type of discussion," she reminded him, her eyes darting here and there, her hands fluttering out to touch on the counters and cabinet doors.

Stone sighed, leaned into the counter. "And tell me one more time why exactly we can't have this type of discussion?"

She looked at him then, the blue of her eyes flashing like the lightning outside the windows. "You know why. And you promised—"

"I've been known to break promises."

"You won't break this one. If you do, I'll have to find another job before I even get started at Stone Enterprises next week."

"Right," he said. Pushing his hands through his hair, he added, "What was I thinking, hiring you?"

"Regrets already?"

"If you weren't coming to work for me, would things be different between us, Tara?"

"Do you mean in a romantic way?"

"A very romantic way."

"I don't know." She turned to stare out into the growing darkness. "I don't think I'm ready for that kind of intensity again."

"Is that how it was with you and Chad? Intense?"

She nodded, wrapped her arms against her midsection. "Intense and impulsive. But it burned itself out in the end."

"Tell me about that."

"You know most of it."

"I want to know all of it."

"Okay, I'll tell you because I want you to understand how things have to be between us. Ana and Chad were dating in college, until I came along. Chad and I fell for each other hard. We broke Ana's heart, but she was gracious enough to let him go so he could be with me. We got married on a whim, our whole relationship based on a physical attraction. And we both regretted that for most of our marriage. And for most of the marriage, I believed my husband was still in love with my sister, and she with him. I was wrong on both counts. Chad died thinking I didn't love him. And it's true. I didn't love him enough to fight for our marriage. So I won't, I can't, rush into another relationship, just because you make me feel—"

"You want more," Stone interjected, at last understanding her completely.

"Yes, I want more. I want a real commitment. I want the kind of love I see when I'm around Ana and

Rock. And I want my children to heal.'' She whirled around just as another clash of thunder and lightning hit the night sky. And then the whole house went black.

"Tara?"

"I'm here," she said. "Perfect timing. A power outage?"

"Looks that way. I plan to have a generator installed, but for now, looks like we're in the dark."

"Yes, for now I think we are."

Stone took that to mean he would still be in the dark about a lot of things. Until she learned to trust him.

"Mom?"

"We're coming, Marybeth. Stay where you are, okay?"

"It's dark."

Stone guided Tara through the maze of the hallways. "We've got flashlights and candles, girls. Hang on."

Amanda giggled. "This is fun."

"Speak for yourself," Laurel said, her tone a mixture of petulance and defiance. "This is dumb. Mom, when can we leave?"

"It's not safe right now," Stone said as they came into the shadowy den. "That rain is really coming down."

Tara could hear the storm pelting the old mansion. "I hope you at least had the roof fixed."

"The roof is intact," Stone said, his reassuring smile showing as he held up a candle they'd found in the kitchen. "And you're all safe right here until this storm passes."

"I want to go home," Laurel said, her hands hitting the arms of the plush leather chair she was slumped into.

"Laurel, how do you expect me to take you home right now?" Tara asked as she and Stone sat down on the long couch beside Marybeth. "Let's just wait until the worst of this storm passes."

"We shouldn't even be here," Laurel said, her harsh words echoing out over the still, high-ceilinged arch of the room.

Tara saw Stone's look of concern in the dim light from the candles he'd placed on the glass coffee table. "Didn't you have a good time today, Laurel?"

Laurel shrugged. "It was okay."

"I'm sorry Cal couldn't stay," Tara said, hoping that would diffuse Laurel's anger.

It didn't. Laurel sat up to glare at her mother. "Yeah, he has to leave, but you get to stay here all nice and cozy with him." She pointed to Stone. "Do you think that's fair, Mom?"

"I think that I'm an adult and I think that you need to speak to me in a more respectful manner."

"You can't even be honest about *him!*" Laurel said, her voice rising just as the rain grew heavier outside. "Don't you understand, we know you're in love with him."

"Laurel!" Tara lifted off the couch to stand over her daughter. "You do not know what you're talking about."

"Yes, I do," Laurel said, getting up to glare at

Tara. "It sure didn't take you long to forget our daddy."

"Laurel," Tara said on a softer voice, her emotions hitting as hard as the storm. "Laurel, how can you say that?"

"It's true," Laurel said, her hands on her hips. "You never loved Daddy. So it's easy for you to forget about him."

Tara sank down onto the sofa, unable to put into words what she needed to say to her daughter. She felt a soft touch on her arm and saw Amanda staring up at her. "Is she right, Mom? You didn't love Daddy?"

"I loved your father," Tara said, the darkness giving her more courage than she felt inside her trembling soul. "We had some problems and we had some terrible fights, but we loved each other. I want all of you to know and remember that."

Marybeth stayed quiet, but Laurel was just getting started. "Then why are you selling our land to *him?* And why are you always with *him?*"

Tara couldn't speak. She stared over at Stone, saw the heat of anger on his face.

"I think I can answer that, if you'll let me," Stone said, his tone so calm and sure that Tara wondered if he'd heard any of the accusations her daughter had just thrown at her.

"Why don't you, then," Laurel said, as if to dare him.

"Okay," Stone replied. He turned off the flashlight so that the big room was illuminated with only the glow from the candles on the table.

Outside, the storm intensified, battering the trees and garden, probably washing away much of the ground cover they'd just planted, Tara thought in a detached way.

"Before I answer your question, Laurel, I want you to do two things for me. First, I want you to sit down and be quiet. And second, I want you to apologize to your mother."

Laurel sat down. "I don't have to apologize," she said, the words hitting Tara like shards of glass.

"Then you won't get any explanations," Stone said.

The room filled with silence. Tara sat wondering what to do now. Did she grab her daughters and leave? Did she turn down every offer Stone had made to her, including the offer of friendship and maybe something more? She knew she would, if it would help her children.

She was about to go, when Laurel finally spoke on a soft, defiant whisper. "I'm sorry, Mom."

"That's better," Stone said. "Now, before I explain things about your mother and me, I want to tell you all a story. Are you willing to sit still and listen until the very end?"

"I will," Marybeth said.

"Me, too," Amanda replied.

"Okay, whatever," Laurel said.

"Good." Stone sat back in the leather wing chair. "I think I'll build a fire with some of the old lumber stacked down in the basement. Let's all get comfortable. This might take a while."

* * *

He didn't know what he was going to say. Stone only knew that Laurel reminded him of himself, in so many ways. And he also knew that Tara was suffering in much the same way his own mother must have suffered. Except Eloise had kept her grief and her suffering to herself and had poured it all out in her art. Her children had needed her, but his mother hadn't known how to offer anything more than obligatory love. He didn't want Tara's girls to feel that way, to feel cut off from the love he saw in Tara's heart. So he had to tell them, had to show them how to heal.

Outside, the thunder and lightning boomed like cymbals, heralding a storm that continued to cover the island in a wash of wind and water. The candles flickered, giving a soft glow to the expectant faces watching him. The fire roared and hissed in the massive fireplace, its yellow sparks casting the old mansion's shadows in a golden hue.

Stone swallowed, said a silent prayer, and hoped he was doing the right thing. He'd never talked about this with anyone. But right now, this very minute, he needed to talk.

The darkness shrouded him in comfort as he cleared his throat. "You all know that I lost my father when I was very young. Tillman Dempsey was my father, and he was a fisherman. He died out there in the ocean in a storm much like this one. We never found his body."

Marybeth gasped, but stayed quiet. Amanda snuggled close to Tara. And Laurel kept her arms wrapped against her stomach and stared at the fireplace.

"But there's more to this story," Stone said, his voice sounding above the din of falling rain. He looked at Tara. "Much more."

"Is this a ghost story? Are you trying to scare us?" Laurel asked in a sarcastic tone.

"No, I'm not trying to scare you," Stone said with a wry smile. "But, yes, there are ghosts in this story. Ghosts from the past, in a figurative sort of way, I suppose."

"You aren't making any sense," Laurel retorted.

"Laurel, please listen," Stone replied before Tara could reprimand her daughter. Then he let out a long sigh. "This isn't easy for me. I'm not a big talker. I don't like to talk about things, especially about my childhood."

Laurel kept glaring at him, but thankfully, remained silent.

"My mother and father fell in love with each other when they were very young, but my mother came from one of the wealthiest families on this island."

"Did they live in a house like this?" Amanda asked, tossing her blond hair.

"They had several houses," Stone said, the old bitterness coloring his words. "They had a nice mansion in Savannah and a summer house here on the island. That's the house my mother still lives in today."

"I love that house," Marybeth said.

Tara put a finger to her lips, her eyes on Stone. "Go ahead," she said, her interest obvious in the way her eyes held his.

"Okay, so they fell in love. My mother told of how he was walking up the beach and she saw him. And she knew that he was the man she would marry.'' Stone stopped, his gaze moving over Tara. ''I used to wonder how she knew that, how she knew just from seeing him that she wanted to spend the rest of her life with him. But now…I think I can understand that concept.''

Tara lowered her gaze, but not before he saw the mixture of fear and awe in her eyes.

''So they got married?'' Marybeth asked, her young voice filled with the same awe he saw in Tara's expression.

''They got married, in spite of her parents' protests. And because of that, her parents disowned her. They didn't think this poor shrimper's son was good enough for their society daughter.''

''But Eloise loved him anyway, didn't she?'' Amanda asked.

''Yes, she did,'' Stone said, the awe coming from his words now. ''She did.'' He sat silent for a while, then said, ''So they lived in the Victorian house by the sea—the house my mother had always loved. She only accepted that one gift from her parents, and it was the only thing they offered, because they rarely came out to the island house. It was always her haven. She accepted nothing more. No money, no friendship, no family holidays together. No communication at all.''

Laurel didn't speak, but Stone saw the furtive look she shot her mother. Maybe she was listening.

''Then they had three children. Three boys.''

''And Eloise named you all funny names,'' Amanda said with a giggle.

"Yes, she did. She gave us strong male names, Roderick, Stanton, and Clayton. Then she gave us nicknames that marked us for life."

"Rock, Stone, and Clay," Marybeth said, grinning. "So keep going, *Stanton*."

Stone grinned back at her. "Now you know why I prefer Stone." He smiled at Tara and was rewarded with a quick, warm smile back.

"Could you get to the point?" Laurel asked, hiding her obvious curiosity behind a cold stare.

"Right, back to the story. Anyway, as we grew up, we heard the stories around the island about the estranged relationship between our parents and my grandparents. We never knew my dad's parents. They died when we were little. But we sure wanted to know our other grandparents. Our mother refused to talk about them, refused to discuss them. Even when they tried to make amends. They wanted us to come and visit them in Savannah. But she wouldn't let us."

"Why not?" This came from Laurel.

Stone gave her his full attention. "At the time, I thought our mother was being mean and selfish. But I think she was trying to protect us. She wanted us to grow up as individuals, to make our own way. She was terrified that her domineering, powerful parents would try to mold us and shape us into something we couldn't be, the same way they'd tried to control her. So we never got to know them."

"Did you ever see them?"

Stone looked over at Marybeth. "Once, I saw them down on the beach. They'd been watching and waiting to see one of us. They saw me and called out to me. How they knew it was me, I'll never know. I talked to them for a long time and they gave me some money. I had to hide the money from my mother, but I never spent it. I saved it and planned on taking it with me when I ran away to make my fortune.''

''Did you run away?'' Laurel asked, all attitude gone now. She sat up, waiting for his answer.

''I tried a few times,'' Stone replied. ''But Rock always found me and brought me home.'' He leaned forward, holding his hands together across his knees. ''Until I went away to college. Then I turned my back on my family for a while. I didn't keep in touch with them the way I should have.''

''You got rich, though,'' Amanda said on a pragmatic note.

Stone nodded. ''I got rich, yes. But—and this is the part I want all of you to listen to very carefully—I came back here and bought this house—a house where I used to work doing odd jobs just to make pocket change. I bought this house thinking I would at last feel some sense of justice, some sense of accomplishment.'' He looked at Tara now. Her eyes were wide and misty. ''But I didn't realize how lonely I was until the day I saw your mother.''

Tara's gaze held his, a look of utter confusion changing to a look of understanding. Almost trust.

''Was it love at first sight, like Eloise and your father?'' Amanda asked.

''It sure was something,'' Stone replied, afraid to voice what he felt in his heart. ''All I can say is this— it changed me.'' Then he looked straight at Laurel. ''So, yes, Laurel, your mother and I have been spend-

ing a lot of time together. You see, I admire your
mother. She's a lot like my mother—a young widow,
struggling to raise a family. But there is one very
distinct difference between Tara and my mother.''

''What's that?'' Laurel asked, the dare back in her
voice.

''Your mother is willing to fight for you. She's
willing to sacrifice for you. She wants you to remember your father—my mother wouldn't even talk about
our father with us. Your mother wants you to stay
close to both of your grandparents—her parents and
Chad's parents. And she's willing to come and work
for me, a man she doesn't trust and maybe doesn't
even respect, for your sake.''

He heard Tara's sharp intake of breath at about the
same time Laurel bolted out of her chair. ''That's
your story? That's what this is all about? She's not
doing this for us. She's doing this because she never
loved our father, and she probably would rather she
didn't have us to worry about! She'd rather work all
day long, than to have to come home to us at night.
And now, she gets to spend time with you at work
and *after* work, too. How fair is that?''

''Laurel, that's not true,'' Tara said.

''It is true, Mom. Before Dad died, you were never
home. And now, it's going to be the same thing.
You'll be with Stone, finding excuses to stay away
from us. Why'd you even bother having children?''

''Laurel, honey, how can you say that to me?''
Tara asked, her voice cracking with hurt and anger.

Laurel was so mad, she didn't bother answering.

Then she took off through the dark. Stone could hear her running down the hallway.

"Laurel?" Tara called, jumping up.

"Let me go," Stone said, grabbing a flashlight. "I know my way around this place. You stay here with Marybeth and Amanda."

He headed up the long central hallway, acutely aware of the construction scaffolding and power tools scattered around the old house. Laurel could get hurt if she wasn't careful.

"Laurel," he called, shining the flashlight down toward the drawing room and library. "Laurel, stop hiding."

He only heard the rain softening to a drizzle outside.

Checking the long drawing room and the dark-paneled library, he found only covered furniture and stored books.

Stone wondered where Laurel would go. The girl didn't know her way around this house. It was full of secret doors and hidden hallways. If something happened to her—

He heard a crash upstairs, near the rear terrace. His heart hammering like an anvil, Stone rushed up to the second floor. "Laurel, are you here? Answer me, right now!"

"I'm over here," came the weak reply.

Stone pointed the flashlight toward the sound of Laurel's voice. "Are you hurt?"

She came out from behind a huge armoire centered near the terrace doors. "No. I think I knocked over a vase or something."

Stone didn't know whether to hug her or give her a piece of his mind. Deciding to stay calm, he thought back on the times he'd done the very same thing to Rock. Running away. Hiding out. Pouting. Blaming. So much bitterness, and for what? No one was to blame for his father's death, just as no one was to blame because his mother had fallen for a poor man and married him. As Stone stood there in the darkness, he had a crystal clear image of what he must have put Rock and his mother through.

He laughed out loud. "Okay, God, I can see you have a strong sense of humor." Or maybe a sense of justice, Stone mused.

"Why are you laughing?" Laurel asked, her voice trembling.

Stone walked toward her, letting the flashlight trail over her to make sure she wasn't hurt or bleeding. "Well, sweetheart, I've just figured out one of life's great lessons."

"Oh, so are you going to fill me in?" She looked small and unsure, but she gave him a defiant glare all the same.

"Yes," Stone said, grabbing her by the arm to bring her into the faint light from the paned doors to the terrace. "I think I'm getting paid back for all my shortcomings. I used to run and hide like this myself, when I didn't want to deal with a situation."

"I don't have to deal with this," Laurel said, trying to pull away. "I don't like you and I don't like how my mother is acting."

Stone held her with a gentle strength. "Really, now. Well, you know something? No one likes the way you're acting, either. Have you ever stopped to think that you're supposed to be the oldest daughter? You're supposed to set a good example for your sisters.''

"I baby-sit them just about every day," the girl retorted.

"That's good. But baby-sitting and being a sister are two different things." He could be noble now, now that he saw his older brother in a whole new light.

"I don't have to listen to you," Laurel said.

"No, you don't."

He stood there, his gaze fixed on her. She tried not to flinch and look away, but finally she gave in. "I guess I was horrible to my mom."

"Yes, you were. You have been for a while now."

"I don't mean to be. It just comes over me sometimes. I can't explain it, except I just want her to know how I feel—inside."

"I know. We're a lot alike, you and me."

"Everybody says you're mean and rude."

"That's right. I can be both. I have been both."

"Me, too."

"We probably need to change our attitudes, don't you think?"

"Well, tonight *you* were nice." She looked up at him then, her big eyes questioning. "Do you love my mom?"

He couldn't tell her what he felt, since he didn't understand it himself. "I don't know. But I'm pretty sure things are headed that way. Don't you want her to be happy?"

She nodded. "Mostly, I just want some answers."

"Don't we all?"

She didn't say anything for a while. Just stood there watching the last of the rain drip away.

Finally, Stone said, "We'd better get back downstairs. Your mother will be worried. But before we go, will you answer me one question? And please, take this from someone who's been there, okay?"

She shrugged.

"How long are you going to go on punishing your mother for things she can't control or change?"

She didn't answer at first, but he saw the lone tear trailing down her face—saw it in the glare from the single light he was holding in his hand. Then her next words hit Stone with all the force of the wind outside. "I just miss the way things used to be. Even when they fought, at least I had them both there. I felt safe. I don't feel safe anymore."

Stone had to swallow the pain radiating through his chest. That was it, exactly. He'd never felt safe after his father had died. He'd felt abandoned.

"Come here," he said. Then he pulled Laurel into his arms. "It's okay to cry."

She did cry, long and hard, and enough to wet the front of his expensive cotton shirt. But Stone didn't mind. He knew exactly how Laurel felt, had felt that same way himself for so many years. And he'd wished a thousand times that someone would have held him and let him cry.

He hadn't let anybody hold him, though, and he hadn't been able to cry, either. Until now.

Chapter Fourteen

Something was very different.

Tara stared at the work of art centered across from her desk in her new office at Stone Enterprises. But she didn't see the abstract work of Salvador Dali. She only saw the darkness, the thunder and lightning, and remembered the fear on her daughters' faces as Laurel had run away in the night at Hidden Hill.

Thanking God once again that her eldest daughter had been found safe and sound, Tara thoughts turned to the man who'd brought Laurel back to her. Stone.

That same man had become increasingly distant and quiet since that dark night a week ago. He'd emerged from the darkness with Laurel, his arm on her daughter's shoulder, guiding her back to safety. But there had been something different about him then. And something was definitely different now.

She almost wished for the old, calculating Stone back. The Stone who flirted with her and made suggestive remarks, while he tried to keep a business-type expression on his face. This Stone was so quiet, so brooding, she wondered if Laurel had told him something horrible and untrue just to make him turn away from her.

But then, Laurel had changed, too. She wasn't as abrupt in her answers. She wasn't as cynical and sarcastic in her words or deeds. Laurel was being dutiful and obedient, cooperative and pleasant. Which scared Tara almost as much as her daughter's rebellious defiance had.

Neither one was talking about what had transpired between them that night at Hidden Hill. Stone had simply brought Laurel back downstairs, then suggested they could probably go home. The storm had passed and Laurel was safe.

Had Stone said something to scare Laurel?

But no, it couldn't be anything like that. Even though it had been obvious that Laurel had been crying at some point, they'd been smiling when they'd come back into the candlelit den that night. Smiling and almost at peace with each other. Stone had even hugged Laurel goodbye.

Tara had heard his soft whisper to her daughter. "Be kind to your mother. And remember, if you ever need me, Laurel, you call me. And that goes for you, too," he'd told Tara.

Then he'd turned and gone back upstairs. Laurel had stared after him with a knowing, secretive look that hinted at a deep understanding. And she'd been very quiet on the way home. They'd both been quiet since then. Too quiet.

Had that one statement been Stone's way of saying goodbye to what might have been? Had his talk with Laurel finally changed the way he felt about Tara? So many questions. So many angles. But no one was talking.

This is what you wanted, she reminded herself.

Tara looked down at the preliminary designs for the new subdivision they planned to build on the land. Hidden Haven.

Why did everything Stone Dempsey own have that word *hidden* in it, she wondered. Maybe because since he'd left Sunset Island, he'd kept a part of himself hidden. Maybe because even now when she knew she had such strong feelings toward him, there was still something about him that was hidden and dark. Which only made Tara want to know him more.

"But you signed on to work, not to daydream about your boss." No complaints there. Her office was plush and her job and salary cushy. She had two assistants to help her with everything from client meetings to learning the ropes within the vast corporate structure of Stone Enterprises. She could get home at a decent hour and spend time with her children. She could pay some of her debts. But since arriving here at the lovely home office, she had yet to come face-to-face with the man who'd hired her.

"I guess this is how he likes to operate," she mused out loud. "Behind the scenes and unattainable."

Well, you did want things this way. How many times would she have to tell herself this was for the best?

Her phone rang, causing Tara to jump. "Hello?"

"Hi, Tara. It's Griffin. Could we possibly meet within the next few minutes?"

"Of course," Tara said.

Griffin, a distinguished man who gave new meaning to the term *Southern gentleman,* had been a lifesaver. He'd guided her through the maze of offices in the lavish downtown Savannah building, teaching her all the things she'd need to know in order to get her work done. Griffin had become the middleman again, between Stone and her. Somehow, she'd managed to get through her first week of work without making a complete mess of things. Except with her new boss. The wall was back up between them, and Tara really wanted to know why.

"What did she say?" Stone asked Griffin Smith an hour later. He was standing at the wide solid glass window of his third floor office, very much aware of the woman on the other side of the building. Too aware.

Griffin sighed, then settled down into a leather chair. "She said that everything looks good and she's ready to discuss the rest of the contracts on the transfer of the property. She said the plans look wonderful and she can't wait to get started." Then Griffin threw down his folder. "It's what the woman didn't say that has me concerned."

Stone centered his gaze on his old friend. "What was that?"

"I can't tell you, since she didn't say," Griffin

pointed out with a wave of his hand. "What's going on between Tara Parnell and you, anyway?"

"Nothing," Stone said too quickly. "Nothing at all."

Griffin's bushy white eyebrows shot up. "Oh, it's like that, is it?"

"What's that supposed to mean?"

Griffin ran a hand down his thick mustache. "It means that for the last few weeks, you seemed to be a changed man, Stone. You actually got out and got involved, in a way I've never seen you get involved before. You seemed happier. But now you're back to your old ways."

"Am I?" Stone knew exactly how he was acting. And it was killing him. But Griffin didn't need to hear that.

"I'm fine, Griffin. So you can report back to Diane that both of you are to mind your own business."

"We're just worried about you."

"No need for worry, but I appreciate your concern. I'm handling things the way they have to be handled. For the good of all involved."

"If you say so." Griffin got up. "Anything else you want me to discuss with Tara—before the gala tomorrow night?"

"No. I think that just about does it. Oh, she is going to make an appearance, right? You did stress to her that I expect her to be there?"

"She understands her obligations, Stone."

"Good, good." Then because he couldn't resist, he asked, "Does she…does she seem happy, working here?"

Griffin pursed his lips, gave his boss a puzzled look. "Why don't you ask her yourself?"

"I have work to do. Just tell me."

"She seems content. She's a hard worker. As I said, she understands her obligations. Diane had to remind her yesterday that we shut down promptly at five o'clock." He shrugged. "Of course, we haven't told her that our boss never goes home. Wouldn't want her to get the wrong idea there."

"That's why I'm the boss," Stone replied. "I get to set my own hours."

He watched Griffin leave the room. *Her obligations.*

Tara was obligated to do his bidding now. She worked for him. As soon as the paperwork went through, he'd own the land he had coveted. He should be happy, full of glee. He'd won. Again.

But what about the woman he coveted?

Stone felt as hollow as the metal-and-steel sculpture he'd had his mother design for the courtyard below. As hollow and as cold. Because he'd won all right, but he still didn't have the thing he wanted most.

He wanted Tara. But he couldn't have her. He'd reached that conclusion completely after consoling her daughter there in the storm. He never wanted to hear that kind of anguish in a child's tears again, and he never, ever wanted to open himself up to that kind of anguish again.

All these weeks, he'd been trying to win her over, but that night he'd realized if he pursued Tara, he'd only hurt Laurel more. And probably Tara, too. And especially himself. He'd promised Tara he wouldn't hurt anyone, but he hadn't considered how easily he could be hurt if she didn't want him. Better to resort to the old, safe, hard-hearted ways. Better for all involved if he stuck to the plan of all work, all the time.

He could see it all so clearly now. He'd hidden his heart away long ago, the day his father had died, the day his mother had turned away in her grief. And in all the time since, he'd relied on material things to bring him happiness. But that was just a sham. He was not happy. And now, Stone didn't know if he could ever find his heart again.

At least, not with Tara Parnell.

"Some habits die hard," he said as he stared at his reflection in the heavy glass protecting him from the outside world.

"What is wrong with my son?" Eloise demanded the next Saturday morning.

Ana and Tara glanced up as she entered the busy kitchen of the tea room. "What's the matter now, and which son, exactly?" Ana asked with a soft smile.

Charlotte and Tina both hurried over to stand beside Ana, their eyes wide, their ears open.

"Are you talking about that big sculpture?" Tina asked, grinning. "The one he's moving—"

"*My* sculpture," Eloise interrupted in a superior tone.

Before she could explain, Charlotte nodded, her brown curly hair bouncing. "I saw it yesterday when I was delivering all those cookies Stone ordered from

Ana for the gala. It's beautiful, Miss Eloise. Where have you been hiding it?''

Eloise waved a bejeweled hand in the air. "I gave that piece to Stone when he graduated college. *The Resurrection,* I call it."

Jackie called from her spot at the computer in the office across the hall. "Are y'all gossiping without me?"

Tina answered in a hurry. "Yeah, get in here if you want to hear."

Jackie came scurrying across the hall. "Did I hear something about one of your sculptures, Miss Eloise?"

Eloise shot her a disapproving look which did nothing to quell Jackie's intense interest. "You have mighty big ears, but yes, we're talking about something I created a few years ago and gave to Stone as a gift."

Tara watched as Ana's eyes widened. "Rock told me about that piece. He said it looks like a cross, but you actually designed it to resemble the old pier by the Broken Pier Restaurant." Shrugging, she said, "We went there on our first date."

Eloise nodded. "That's right, dear. It represents a resurrection. It's made of metal and stone, with a waterfall shooting out of the center to represent everlasting life. I made it in honor of my late husband, Till."

The room grew quiet until Tara asked, "What has Stone done with it? Isn't it in the back gardens at Hidden Hill?"

"No," Tina said, her brown eyes widening. "It's—"

Eloise held up a hand. "He's had it put right by the lighthouse. Quite ingenious, really. Every time anyone stares out to sea from just about any hill or bluff on this island, they will not only see the lighthouse restored to its former glory, but they will see the sculpture centered on the rocks and pilings there beside the lighthouse."

Ana quirked her brows. "But Rock told me Stone kept that sculpture hidden away at the mansion. In storage."

"It was in storage," Eloise said, her silver eyes centering on Tara as she talked to Ana. "It was packed up in the garage. Stone said he planned on placing it in the back garden by the pool."

"Guess he changed his mind," Charlotte said just before hurrying off to fill the orders at her tables.

Tina looked from one sister to the other, then back to Eloise. "Maybe Stone decided it was time to bring The Resurrection out of hiding."

"Maybe," Eloise said, her eyes still on Tara.

Ana motioned to Tina to get back to work and the petite woman scurried away, her eyes still wide as she called over her shoulder, "I'll bet Greta Epperson will get to the bottom of this. She's covering the gala, you know."

"We know," Ana and Tara replied at the same time.

Jackie nodded, her chestnut hair touching on her blouse. "She's been snooping around all week, asking about the menu and the entertainment. She's gonna love this.'' She glanced up to find Ana giving her a keen look. ''And I love my job, so I'm going back to my bookkeeping.''

Eloise kept looking at Tara, making Tara acutely aware that she'd either made Stone's mother very angry about something, or Eloise didn't approve of her at all.

But Eloise's question to her changed that assumption.

''What have you done to him—for him?''

Tara pushed at her hair. ''What do you mean?''

''I mean,'' Eloise said, waving her hands in the air, ''that this is a major step, a very interesting change, in my son's attitude. You see, I always thought giving him the sculpture would somehow make up for the way I responded to his father's death, the way I retreated behind my work. But Stone took the sculpture and hid it away, I think to punish me. If he's willing to bring it out and share it with everyone who visits this island, then my dear, that is a big deal. A very big deal. And I can only assume you had something to do with it.''

Not knowing how to answer, Tara glanced over at Ana. ''I don't know…I don't think I did. Stone never mentioned to me what he was going to do with the sculpture, except that he planned to center it behind the pool.''

''It's not going behind the pool,'' Eloise replied. ''He's put it out there for all the world to see.''

Tara heard the implications of that statement. If

Stone was willing to bring the sculpture out of hiding, maybe that meant he was coming out of hiding, too?

Then why on earth was he hiding from Tara?

"You look so pretty," Ana told Tara later that night. "Are you ready?"

Tara stared at her reflection in the oval standing mirror of one of Ana's bedrooms. She'd decided to get ready for the gala here with her sister, to help calm her jangled nerves. The girls were safe at the cottage with Josiah and his daughter to watch out for them. "I think I'm ready," she said as she patted the chignon she'd had done at the local hairdresser's this morning. "How does my dress look?"

Ana's gaze moved over the billowing white satin trimmed with a thick span of black across the low portrait collar. "You look stunning. The black contrast around your shoulders is perfect. And I love the way that black bow falls down your back. Stone won't be able to move or breathe when he sees you."

"I didn't dress for Stone," Tara said as she adjusted the pearl-and-diamond brooch she'd placed against the black satin on her left shoulder. But she immediately knew that wasn't true. She'd dressed with Stone in mind, all right.

"Yes, you did," Ana said, echoing her thoughts as she tugged at her own pink sequined formal. "But that's to be expected. He is your boss now. And you don't want to make the boss mad."

"But he is mad, I think," Tara admitted. "Ana, the man hasn't said two words to me since I started work on Monday."

Ana stood silent for a minute, her dainty diamond

earrings sparkling underneath her upswept hair. "Isn't that how you wanted things, honey?"

Tara sank down on the four-poster bed, not caring if she crushed her full-skirted ball gown. "Yes, and no. I wanted him to stop pressuring me, but I fully expected him to at least act professional around me."

"Well, isn't being cold and distant Stone's professional mode of operation?"

"Yes, it *was,* from everything I'd heard. But he never acted that way toward me. Until now. I thought we could at least be friends. What if he regrets hiring me?"

"Have you given him any reason to regret anything?"

Tara thought back over the last week. "No. He started acting strange after he found Laurel upstairs at Hidden Hill. I think they must have had some sort of heart-to-heart talk. Laurel won't tell me anything and Stone won't even come near me."

Ana touched a hand to her hair. "Do you think Laurel said something mean and vindictive to him? I mean, that has been *her* MO lately."

Tara got up and grabbed her matching black-and-white satin wrap. "No, I don't think it was that. Laurel would have boasted about that if she'd done it. She's been so quiet, so nice. It's almost as if she finally understands about her father's death."

"Maybe Stone talked to her—he has been through the same experience. And maybe talking to her brought all of that back for him. The man seems to be struggling with letting go. Once he works through that, I think he'll come around."

"Do you think it could be that?" Tara asked, hopeful even as her heart told her not to count on it. If Stone and Laurel had compared notes, then whatever they'd discussed obviously hadn't helped Stone. He seemed miserable now.

"I think anything is possible," Ana said, smiling at their reflections as they checked their dresses one more time. "Maybe you'll get a chance to talk to Stone tonight and find out what really happened."

"Maybe," Tara said as they headed down to where Rock was waiting to drive them to the gala. Then she stopped at the landing. "Remember when you were so afraid of loving Rock?"

Ana nodded. "I finally had everything I'd ever wanted and I was still scared to accept it."

"I think I've reached that point," Tara replied, her voice low. "I finally have a great job, I can pay off my debts. I've even managed to sell that land, just as I'd hoped. But I'm afraid to take the next step. I'm waiting for the other shoe to fall. It just seems as if…something is still missing."

"Is that something Stone Dempsey?" Ana asked.

"I don't know. I think maybe I'm afraid of being hurt again, or that if I let my feelings for Stone show, I'll mess things up with my children."

"But if you don't try," Ana said, "you'll never know the joy of love again. You and Stone might be able to overcome all of that, Tara."

Tara nodded. "I needed some time. Maybe I still do. But I want to know where I stand with Stone. I want to know if he even considers me a friend still."

Ana patted her arm. "Talk to him, then. Remember, I went after Rock and found out he thought he was doing me a favor by walking away. He was wrong, so wrong. And I'm sure glad I did go after him, or we might not be together today. You know how men can be. They clam up and refuse to tell us how they really feel.''

''But with Stone, it's the exact opposite,'' Tara said. ''He was very honest about things and now he's shut down, and I don't have any explanations.''

''Talk to him,'' Ana urged. ''Maybe he'll be honest with you again, if you're up front with him.''

Tara didn't know if she could go after Stone, not after she'd pushed him away so many times. But she had to find out what had brought about this swift change in him. She had to find out why he was acting so indifferent toward her. If he couldn't love her, at least she wanted him to know she could be his friend and work with him at Stone Enterprises. But when she thought about the last week and how distant he'd become, Tara wondered how she'd ever live up to that pledge.

When Tara and Ana rounded the stairs, they found Rock waiting in the hallway for them, his expression full of surprise. ''My brother sent a limo for us.''

''A limo?'' Ana asked, giggling like a school girl. ''I've got to hand it to him, the man has style.''

Rock looked affronted. ''And what was wrong with going to the gala in my old van?''

''Nothing, sweetheart,'' Ana replied, realizing her mistake. ''I'll be glad to let you escort me to the gala in your battered old vehicle, if it will make you feel better.''

Rock sighed, then grinned. "Are you kidding? I've never ridden in a limo."

"You don't mind?" Ana asked, smiling.

"Of course not," Rock said. "This is my brother's fancy affair. If he wants to send a limo for us, so be it. It's for a good cause, right?"

"Right," Ana said as she turned to Tara. "And how do you feel about this?"

"I'm not sure," Tara said, a sinking feeling in the pit of her stomach. "I just don't know what Stone is up to now."

Rock nodded. "He likes to keep people guessing."

"Do you want to go in your car?" Ana asked.

"No," Tara replied. "He might be offended if his newest employee refuses his kind gesture." Then she turned to Rock. "And I like limos, too."

Rock opened the front door for them. "That means you've ridden in one before, huh?"

"A few times, when Chad was trying to impress someone," she said, remembering how pretentious she'd felt. "It is fun to pretend to be rich, though."

Rock led them down to the driver standing beside the sleek white car. "Well, obviously my brother doesn't have to pretend. He really is a wealthy man."

Ana held a hand on her husband's arm. "Does that still bother you?"

Rock stared at the car, then looked back at his wife. "Not like it used to. Not as long as he learns to use his wealth in a positive way, such as tonight."

"I love you," Ana said, reaching up to kiss her husband on the cheek.

"Even if I don't own a limo?" Rock teased.

"I think *because* you don't own a limo," Ana replied.

"I love you, too," Rock said, grinning. "But mainly because *you* own a tea room."

Ana playfully tapped his arm. "So you married me for my muffins?"

Rock gave his wife an appreciative look. "Oh, yeah."

Tara stood back, watching the sweet scene, and wishing she could feel that kind of solid love in her own heart.

Then she thought of Stone and how cold he'd been lately. Even when she'd denied wanting anything more than a working relationship with Stone, she'd hoped. She'd thought—but her heart was so bruised. Now she knew there might not be a chance for her to ever feel that way again.

At least, not with Stone Dempsey.

Some fears never go away, she thought as she got into the shiny limo that would take her to him.

Chapter Fifteen

The gardens at Hidden Hill were illuminated with thousands of tiny white lights that stretched out like a woman's lace shawl across the trees and bushes. A huge white tent filled with chairs and tables and buffets of food had been set up just beyond the now clean and sparkling swimming pool. The pool itself was filled with fragrant water lilies and floating candles that made the water look alive as they moved with the swirling current.

Up on the first-floor terrace, an orchestra played, the cello, flutes, harps, and violins sending the soft, haunting music out over the trees and flowers like butterflies lifting in delicate sound.

Tara stood near the pool, her eyes scanning the impressive crowd of both Sunset Island's and Savannah's finest citizens. She was looking for their absent host, Stone Dempsey. He had yet to make an appearance at his own party.

"Seen him yet?" Rock asked from her side, then handed her a crystal goblet of sparkling mineral water with a twist of lime.

"No," Tara said, not even bothering to deny it. "I wish I knew what's going on inside his head."

Rock chuckled. "Get in line. We've all been wanting to know that for a very long time."

She turned to stare over at Rock. He looked distinguished in his tuxedo. He was handsome in a different way than Stone. Rock's handsomeness was rugged and straightforward, whereas Stone's was mysterious and distant. Hidden away. "But you and Stone—you've made your peace, right?" she asked, worry causing her to whisper the question.

"Yes, I think we finally have," Rock said. "And I have you and Ana to thank for that. Ana made me see that I needed to reach out to my brother, and you made me see that I'd been judging him too harshly."

Tara nodded, pulled her wrap closer around her shoulders. "I truly think he's been out there all alone for so long that he expects to be judged. He almost welcomes it as a challenge, maybe to keep his bitterness brewing."

Rock chuckled again. "You Hanson women never cease to amaze me. You are both so wise."

"Not wise," Tara said, shaking her head. "We've just learned our lessons the hard way."

"Well, you two had some issues to sort through yourselves," Rock reminded her. "And now you're closer than ever."

Tara smiled, took a sip of the tingling water. It soothed her dry throat. "Yes, and I have *you* to thank for that. You encouraged me to turn back to God, to turn it all over to Him. It seems to be working.''

Rock raised his own glass. ''And it seems we have a mutual admiration society going here.''

Tara agreed, then toasted him in return. ''Now, if we could just get your brother on track, we'd really have something to celebrate.''

Rock took a drink, then nodded. ''Give him time, Tara. It took him many years to build up that wall. It might take a while for us to tear it down. Remember that saying by Edwin Markham, something about 'he drew a circle that shut me out…but love and I had the wit to win. We drew a circle that took him in'?''

Tara bobbed her head, glanced out at the sea. ''I've heard it before, yes.''

''I think we need to do that with Stone,'' Rock said. ''I think he's shut himself down again because he's come close to finding everything that he's been missing in life.''

''And he's afraid?'' Tara asked. ''You think he's walking away from me before it's too late?''

Rock nodded in silence. ''Stone's never opened his heart to anyone. Then you came along and you were the one. That's got to be scaring him to death.''

''I know the feeling.'' Tara looked down at the shimmering pool. ''Me, I tried to give my heart to my husband and my children, but it wasn't enough. I didn't know how to love enough, Rock. I'm not sure if I'll ever know that feeling again, or what a complete love is really like.''

Rock pointed toward the starlight sky. ''Trust in Him, Tara. That's all I can tell you. That's what complete love is—it's more than just physical or more than just a passing infatuation. It takes commitment, work, and most of all, it takes putting God into the relationship.''

''Thanks,'' Tara said. ''And speaking of a complete love, go and dance with your wife.''

''Good idea,'' Rock replied with a silly grin.

Tara stood there looking around at the crowd, her gaze moving over the sequined evening gowns and expensive tuxedoes, her ears hearing the clutter of mindless chatter, while her heart was clamoring to run to Stone, find him, tell him she wanted to see inside his battered heart.

What should I do, Lord? she silently asked the heavens. *I made such a mess of things with Chad. We didn't love each other enough to fight for what we needed to save our marriage. I didn't nurture him enough to save him. And now he's gone and my daughters are suffering. I'm suffering, God. I don't want to make the same mistake with Stone. But he needs me. He needs someone to show him what real love means, the way You showed us with Your son. Lord, do I dare tell Stone what's in my heart?*

A noise behind her caused her to whirl around, hopeful. It wasn't Stone. ''Laurel?'' Tara squinted as her daughter sprinted down the steps. ''What are you doing here, honey?''

''I snuck out,'' Laurel replied. Then she came rushing toward Tara. ''Mom, don't be mad, please. Josiah said I needed to talk to you. But I couldn't wait until you got home.''

Fear gripping her heart, Tara said, "What's wrong, Laurel?"

Laurel stood in her jeans and zippered pink fleece jacket, her golden hair shimmering on her shoulders. "Mom, I'm sorry."

"Sorry for what, sweetie?"

"For being so mean to you. Josiah told me everything, about how my daddy came out to the chapel, about how Daddy wanted to love us, but he didn't know how to show it. Josiah said the fighting wasn't anyone's fault. He said Daddy was a very sick man, and a very confused man, but he told me Daddy found God before he died."

"Oh, baby," Tara said, pulling Laurel onto a long stone bench and then into her arms. "Baby, you didn't have to come all the way over here to tell me that."

"But I needed you to know, I understand now," Laurel said. "Stone and me, we had a long talk here the other night. He told me how he'd blamed his mother for a lot of things and how he regretted being so mad all the time. He said that if God gives us another chance to find love, we should listen to our hearts and take that chance. He wanted me to understand that *you* needed a second chance."

"Stone told you that?"

Laurel nodded, wiped at her eyes. "But he told me he wouldn't cause me any more pain, either. He told me he'd leave you alone until I was ready to understand and accept things between you two." She pushed at her hair, then wiped at her eyes. "I think I'm ready now, Mom. Josiah read to me from the

Bible, about Cain and Abel, the prodigal son, about Naomi and Ruth, all these stories of forgiveness and love. I've been so mean, Mom. I didn't want Stone to take my Daddy's place. But Josiah said Stone isn't supposed to do that. He said Stone needs us, just as much as we need him. Josiah said God brought all of us together for a reason. And after talking to Stone and really seeing how he feels, I think Josiah is right. So, I'm sorry. You've tried so many times to explain things to me, but I've been so angry and mean. I'm really sorry, Mom.''

"Oh, Laurel." Tara pulled her daughter close, rocking her gently. "I love you so much, baby. I promise I'm going to make this up to you, somehow. And if that means giving up Stone—''

Laurel pulled back, sniffing away the last of her tears. "No, you have to tell Stone, Mom. You have to tell him that I'm okay now—that I understand. He won't come back to us unless he hears it from you— he told me that.''

Tara nodded, seeing why Stone had pulled away over the last week. He'd done it for Laurel, to show her daughter that he cared enough to walk away. And he'd probably decided he couldn't bear the pain of rejection if Tara or Laurel never accepted him. The same pain he'd suffered since childhood, that numbing pain that had caused him to turn away from love and his family.

How could she not accept a man who'd do that for her child? The respect and trust Stone had tried so hard to gain was evident now. And now, Tara knew without a doubt that she loved him.

God had answered her prayer.

Tara sat there on the secluded stone bench near the terrace of Hidden Hill, and talked to her daughter for a very long time. And she explained everything to Laurel, from the beginning. Then she sent her daughter back to the cottage, trusting that Laurel would find her way home. Her oldest daughter had matured into a caring young woman.

After Laurel left, Tara stood listening to the music, to the wind, to the sea. She heard all the sounds of God's world here on this island, but she waited to hear the sound of Stone's footsteps coming toward her.

She waited, but he didn't come. Which meant she'd just have to go and find him.

He couldn't bring himself to go out there and find her.

Stone stood in the middle of the solarium, looking at the rows and rows of orchids he'd grown himself. He wanted to give one particularly beautiful lady's slipper to Tara, but fear gripped him like fish netting and he felt trapped in the darkness of his own doubts. Trapped here in the solarium, behind glass and flowers.

While the band played on.

"What are you doing?"

Stone whirled to see Eloise standing in the arched doorway. "How did you find me?" he asked in answer to her question.

"I wandered around until I did," his mother replied. "You have guests, son."

"Yes, I know. And I have a well-paid staff to see to all their needs."

"Don't want to get too personal with your donors and patrons?"

"The money is for the lighthouse, Mother, not me."

"But you need to show your gratitude. Your benefit gala is a rousing success."

"Then everyone should be pleased."

Eloise walked further into the room, her burgundy wrinkled silk gown rustling like fallen leaves. "Stone, I'll ask again—what are you doing?"

"I'm hiding," he said, not caring what she thought about his actions. "And I'd like to be alone."

Then he heard his mother's gasp, and turned to see what was wrong. He watched as her eyes scanned the orchids.

"Oh, my," Eloise said, waving a hand. "So many colors, so many varieties. Stone, who brought in these orchids?"

"I did," he said simply and quietly, while his heart hammered a roar to equal the cresting waves down below the bluff.

"Well, who's your supplier?"

Stone shook his head, put his hands in the pockets of his tuxedo pants. "I grew these myself, Mother. I take care of them myself. They're mine."

Eloise walked closer, the muted light from the hanging art deco chandelier making her face glisten. "You grew these?"

"Yes." He didn't feel the need to explain.

But then, his mother, ever full of surprises, gave

him the shock and the thrill of his life. "I remember you tried to grow an orchid for me once, for Mother's Day. You wanted it to bloom so badly."

"But it never did," Stone said, his voice catching under the roughness of that memory. He stood silent for a couple of beats, then said, "How did you know about that? Did Rock tell you?"

Eloise turned to him then, her hand touching on his face with the gentleness of an artist touching a work in progress. "No one had to tell me, Stone. I knew it back then. And I remember it now. I was always there, son, listening."

Stone took in a breath to push away the lump in his throat. "But you never said anything, never responded."

"No, not in the way you needed me to. I'm responding now, though." She held her hand to his face, her eyes holding his. "Will you forgive me?"

Stone didn't push her hand away. It felt so warm there on his skin. "Do you know, Mother, there are certain orchids that can actually survive growing on rock? They're called lithophytes."

"Yes, I've heard of them. Amazing that they just need rain and humidity to make them thrive."

"They stick to the rocks, but they can't gain sustenance unless it rains, and yet they stay attached anyway, waiting for the water to come."

"Waiting for the rain to nurture them," Eloise replied. Then she dropped her hand and reached out her arms to her son. "I'm here now, Stone. And I'm so very glad you stayed attached. Because I have never let go."

Stone hugged his mother close, savoring the feel of being in the arms of another human being. Then he stood back and took a long breath. "I'm in love, Mother."

"I know, son."

"What should I do?"

"You should go find her and tell her."

"What if—"

Eloise quieted him with a finger to his lips. "What if you don't? We all know there are no promises and no guarantees in life, except that of God to man."

"I guess God is a lot like my lithophytes."

Eloise smiled. "He sticks to us, even when we don't want to allow His love to break through."

"I remembered something the other night," he told her. "My father was a true Christian. He was a fisher of men."

Eloise inhaled a sharp breath, her eyes glistening. "Yes, he was."

Stone ran a hand through his long bangs. "All these years, I've been mourning how he died, when I should have been honoring how he lived."

"If you can do that, darling, you will indeed be your father's son."

They stood silent for a few minutes, the sounds of the distant music drifting up to them, the soft cease-less waves of the sea comforting them.

"Okay," Stone said. "I've wasted enough time."

Eloise kissed him on the cheek. "Good then. Oh, and Stone, *The Resurrection* looks perfect down on the rocks. Your father would be so proud."

"That's why I put it there," he said. "Pick yourself out an orchid, Mom. And…Happy Mother's Day."

Then he turned and went in search of Tara.

"Are you sure?" Ana asked Tara later.

Ana and Rock were ready to go home, but Tara wanted to stay. She had to talk to Stone.

"I'll be fine," she said, her hand on her sister's arm. "I can call a cab or have that fancy limo drop me off."

"Okay, then," Ana said, worry evident in the expression on her face. "Tell Stone we had a lovely time. Sorry we missed him."

"I will." Tara looked around the grounds. The orchestra was still playing, but most of the guests had gone home. It was late, but the question on everyone's mind had been the same. Where was Stone Dempsey?

"Greta Epperson is even giving up," Rock commented as the blond, bespectacled society page reporter stomped past them with a haughty look, her notebook still in hand just in case the mysterious Mr. Dempsey decided to put in an appearance.

"Well, thank goodness for that," Tara replied. "The woman hounded me all night. I told her about our plans out at Hidden Haven, but Greta only wanted to know what personal plans I had in store with Stone. I couldn't answer that question."

Ana was about to respond, when she looked past Tara. "Uh, can I help you, sir?"

Tara turned to find a formally dressed waiter standing there. He motioned to Tara. "I'm to escort Mrs. Parnell to the dining table."

"Excuse me?" Tara said, wondering what was going on.

"Mr. Dempsey requests your presence at a private dinner, ma'am," the spiffy waiter said with an elegant bow.

"Oh, my, oh, my," Ana said, a smile splitting her face. "I guess it is time for us to go home, Rock."

"Can't we stay and watch? Things are just about to get interesting," Rock said in a mock whine.

Tara looked from the expectant face of the waiter back to her sister and Rock. "What should I do?"

"Do?" Ana pushed at her arm. "Do what you've been wanting to do all night, Tara. Go and talk to Stone."

Tara nodded, her throat too dry to speak. Then she turned back to Ana. "Will you check on Laurel and the girls?" She'd already told Ana and Rock about Laurel's visit.

"Of course," Rock said. "We'll even bring them back to our house, if that will make you feel better."

Tara nodded. "I think Laurel would appreciate that."

She waited until they walked around to the portico on the side of the house, then turned back to the smiling waiter. "I'm ready."

Stone wasn't sure if he was ready for this. But it was now or never. He'd tried to stay away from Tara. He'd even asked God to help him. He'd promised

Laurel he wouldn't hurt her or her mother. But mostly, Stone didn't want to be hurt himself.

But he knew that if he didn't tell Tara that he loved her, he'd become the same miserable excuse of a man he'd been up until now. And he didn't want to be that man anymore.

Stone stood on the sandy beach, just a few feet away from the pounding surf, and looked up the path toward the imposing mansion. To his right, stood the lighthouse. And just beyond that on his left, the stark image of his mother's sculpture shot up into the night from the rocks to meet the stars. Stone could see the water falling gently from the center of the never-ending fountain that his mother had placed in the middle of the steel crossbeams. He'd had the water pipe especially installed among the rocks so the water would always continue to flow out and back into the sea, only to return time and time again, just like the ocean waves.

He'd had a table set up here between the lighthouse and the sculpture. A storm lantern for atmosphere and an orchid for his lady. Dinner for two.

And now he waited for Tara to come. And asked God to show him how to be the man she needed him to be.

Then he saw her. She was walking down the path toward him, her white dress shimmering like bits of moonlight, her wrap falling away from her dainty shoulders, her hair coming out in strands around her face as the tropical wind played through it. The sight of her took his breath, but knowing she was coming to him at last gave him courage.

His heart felt open and full, overflowing, as it sputtered and puttered to a new beat, to a new beginning. He felt a solid wall of fear, but he also felt as if he'd been washed clean and reborn. He couldn't mess up this time.

So he stood there in his tuxedo and held out his hand to the woman he loved.

"You," she said, her expression full of confusion and hope.

"Me," he answered, remembering the first time they'd said those words to each other in such a different way.

Tara nodded, one hand going up to push hair off her face. "I had to see you."

"And I wanted to see you." Stone guided her to one of the high-backed chrome chairs placed at the round, white-clothed table. Then he motioned to the lush bright-pink-and-white flower sitting in a weighted pot on the table. "I brought you this."

"It's lovely."

"It made me think of you."

"Orchids? I remind you of orchids?"

"You're dainty and very ladylike, yes. And a bit exotic, hard to read. You need lots and lots of nurturing."

She smiled and looked down at the table. "Did you have this shipped in just for me?"

"No, I grew this just for you. With my own two hands."

Her head shot up, her gaze touching on him, on his hands. "You always manage to surprise me."

Stone wanted to kiss her. "Are you hungry, thirsty?"

Tara sank down in the chair and allowed him to push it forward on the soft sand. "No, Stone, I'm mostly curious. Where were you all night?"

"I was around," he said, suddenly nervous.

"But you didn't bother to make an appearance."

"No, I didn't. I don't like parties."

"Then why did you throw one?"

"Just to see you in that dress."

"Well, I've been in this dress all night. But I didn't see you."

"I was around," he repeated, remembering how he'd watched her getting out of the limo earlier. Remembering how he'd watched her laughing and smiling as she moved through the crowd. Remembering while he'd watched her that he'd promised to be patient, that he'd promised Laurel he would cause them no more pain. Remembering that he couldn't deal with his own pain. "I saw you, but I couldn't—"

"You couldn't break your promise to my daughter," Tara said as she pushed her wrap away, her eyes locking with his.

"What promise would that be?" he asked with a nonchalant shrug as he settled back in his own chair.

"The one she explained to me tonight, when she came here to tell me that she loves me and she wants me to fight for you. The one you made to her the night she hid in the darkness of your house up there on the hill."

"What about it?"

"What about it?" she repeated, her voice catching

with a mixture of awe and frustration. "You were willing to walk away? You were willing to stay away, for the sake of my children? You'd do that for Laurel?"

Stone felt trapped, like a bit of flotsam caught between the tide and the shore. Almost home. Almost there. He just had to hold on. "I was willing to do whatever I had to do—to make you happy."

She didn't speak. She was scaring him to death. But then he looked over at her and saw a single tear glistening down her cheek. "Tara?"

"Laurel wants us to be together, Stone."

He closed his eyes, tried to breathe. "And how do *you* feel about that?"

"I'm happy," she said, the tears falling freely now. "So happy."

"Because I walked away, or because you're here with me?"

"Both," she said, bobbing her head. "Stone, I respect you so much for what you did. And I trust you. I will never doubt you again."

Stone felt the jagged-edged release of the last crumblings of the wall around his heart. Then a feeling of complete freedom, of complete joy, burst forth inside him, causing him to reach up a hand and clutch it to his chest. "Do you trust me enough to marry me?"

She sat still, her eyes big and blue and as vast as the ocean. The sea crashed at the shore. The wind touched on the trees. The moon laughed at the stars. And Stone knew he'd been put on earth just to reach this moment in his life.

"Yes," she said finally. "Yes, I do." Then she held up a hand. "I thought this was just physical, just a passing infatuation. I didn't want to rush into anything, the way I did with Chad. But Stone, I've never felt this way before. This is so overwhelming, so scary, I've tried to deny it, to hide it."

Stone came out of his chair to pull her into his arms. He crushed her close, his lips touching on her eyes, her hair, her mouth. "No more hiding."

"No, no more hiding," she said as she pushed her hands through his hair to bring his head down to hers. "We're free now, Stone. Free and clear."

Stone held Tara there on the beach, with the ocean waves breaking around them, and knew that he'd come out of the darkness at last. Then he grabbed the lantern off the table and took her by the hand, pulling her along the shore. "I want to show you something."

Tara laughed, followed him to the sculpture called *The Resurrection.* "Read this," he said, holding the lantern so she could see. "It's Psalms 107, Verse 23."

Tara read the King James verse he'd had inscribed in stone at the foot of *The Resurrection:*

"'They that go down to the sea in ships, that do business in great waters; These see the works of the Lord, and his wonders of the deep.'"

She touched a hand on his arm. "You dedicated this to your father—Tillman Dempsey."

"Yes. I understand now, Tara."

Tara turned back into his arms. "Oh, Stone. I never knew I could love this way."

"Me, either," he said. Then he held a hand to her face. "And I never knew I could be loved."

"It's a wonder," Tara said. Then she kissed him again.

Stone accepted that wonder into his heart and felt the joyous burden of happiness and hope and resurrection, at last.

Sunset Island Sentinel Society News
Reported by Greta Epperson

This whole island is all abuzz with news of the upcoming nuptials of none other than that elusive bachelor millionaire Stone Dempsey and the lovely mother of three girls, Tara Parnell. Tara is sister to our own Ana Dempsey, who runs Ana's Tea Room and Art Gallery and is married to Rock Dempsey.

But that's not the best part, oh, no, my friends. This intimate wedding will not take place here on the island, but rather on a spot of land near the Savannah River, in a little chapel in the marsh that apparently holds special memories for the bride and groom.

And there's more. It seems the land, which once belonged to Tara Parnell and her deceased husband, Chad, was sold to Stone Dempsey and slated to be turned into a swank residential development, until Stone and Tara became fast friends with Josiah Bennett, a man who's lived on the land all of his life, was married, and raised four children out there in the marsh. Because of Josiah, Stone Dempsey decided to scrap the idea of a gated community. Instead, he was happy to present his bride-to-be with the plans for just one house out near the marsh—a lovely, rambling, hideaway cottage for his new family.

"I did it for Tara," Mr. Dempsey told me in an exclusive interview I had with the happy couple just this week. "And I did it for Josiah. He wants to stay there to take care of the chapel, and now he will have someone close to take care of him. And besides, Tara and the girls love that spot of land—it was a special place to Tara's late husband, Chad Parnell. I couldn't take that away from them."

And what's to become of Hidden Hill, Stone Dempsey's infamous mansion on the hill here at Sunset Island?

"We're turning it into a grand hotel," Tara Parnell explained. "We want people to enjoy the luxury and history of the house and gardens and to feel free to explore the newly renovated West Island Lighthouse and the rest of Sunset Island. We hope to bring more tourists to the island, and help the economy, too. We've also set up a trust for the lighthouse—for upkeep and continuing restoration."

And where will the happy couple reside?

"We have a suite at Hidden Hill," Tara said, "but we'll probably spend most of our time at our new home back near Savannah, on the river."

I asked if they liked the seclusion out there.

"No," Mr. Dempsey replied, his eyes glowing as he looked at his bride. "We like the openness of the land. We want to be together, but we don't want to hide away from the world."

Well, folks, when Stone Dempsey decided to come

out of hiding, he certainly did it in a huge way. Who knew the man had such a big heart? He's asked his brother Rock to perform the marriage ceremony, and his brother Clay to be his best man. Josiah Bennett will give a special blessing at the wedding, too. I'll be sure to give a thorough wedding report.

And I hope to get an interview with handsome but shy Clay Dempsey when he takes a break from his K-9 police duties in the big city of Atlanta, for an extended vacation here on the island this fall.

Details to follow very soon...

Dear Reader,

I truly enjoyed writing this story of a man who showed the world his heart of stone, while he longed for a heart of flesh. Sometimes, it takes meeting one special person to change us and make us see that we need to turn back to God for our salvation.

In the moment when Stone met Tara, he saw the man he had become. But after getting to know Tara and her girls, he also saw the man he wanted to be. This is what love and marriage and faith are all about. Love and marriage mean we're willing to make a lifelong commitment to another human being, so that the two parts can become a whole in the eyes of God. And having faith means that we're willing to put God first in all of our relationships.

At times we're all like Stone. We harden our hearts to God's love and redemption. We harden our hearts to the people who love us, our families and friends. I hope this story will touch your heart and open it to the possibility of God's immense love and grace. And I hope you'll join me for the next story in the Sunset Island series, when Rock and Stone's younger brother, Clay Dempsey, returns to Sunset Island, to find some rest and redemption of his own, in *A Tender Touch,* available in September 2004. And in May 2004, look for my Steeple Hill single title *After the Storm,* a love story about new beginnings, set in the Blue Ridge Mountains of Georgia.

Until next time, may the angels watch over you—always.

Lenora Worth

AN HONEST LIFE

BY

DANA CORBIT

Charity Sims had been raised to be the perfect preacher's wife—but the one man who intrigued her was the one man her mother didn't approve of: contractor Rick McKinley. Charity was determined to make the loner a churchgoer. And Rick was the one person Charity could count on when her life was shattered by a devastating truth....

Don't miss

AN HONEST LIFE
On sale December 2003

Available at your favorite retail outlet.

LIAHL

Love Inspired

THE CHRISTMAS CHILDREN

BY

IRENE BRAND

All Carissa Whitmore wanted for Christmas was to regain her faith—what better town than Yuletide to find the holiday spirit in? She hadn't planned on sharing the holidays with her friend's brother, Paul Spencer, or the motherless family hiding out in town. Could the miracle of love bring the joy of the season back to Carissa…and give her the family she'd always longed for?

Don't miss

THE CHRISTMAS CHILDREN
On sale December 2003

Available at your favorite retail outlet.